MY FATHER AND MY TWO LOVES

MIRYAM M. ROCHE

My Father
And My Two Loves

MANCHESTER PUBLISHING INC.
HONOLULU

MY FATHER AND MY TWO LOVES

Manchester Publishing Inc.
300 Wai Nani Way, Suite 2311
Honolulu, Hawaii 96815
Phone: 1-808-349-9432
e-mail: manchesterpublishing@yahoo.com
www.manchesterpublishing.com

Manufactured in the United States of America

First Edition

Library Of Congress Control Number: 2012917437

ISBN 978-1-940273-10-5

E-book ISBN 978-0-9855775-8-2

Interior design by Ariana Fernandez

ACKNOWLEDGMENTS

I thank my family for helping me to write this novel, especially my mother, sisters, brothers, relatives and all my friends.
I dedicate this book to my father that our Lord Jesus Christ bless him in peace and happiness in Heaven.

BIOGRAPHY OF THE AUTHOR

Miryam Muñoz Roche, Chilean North American writer, was born in Chillán, Chile and was educated at a Catholic school and at the Catholic University in Santiago, where she majored in English literature. Then, she went to study at Cambridge University, England, where she switched majors, starting her studies in psychology. She graduated with a B.A, M.A, and a PhD in Clinical Psychology. She also has a B. A and a M. A. in English and French Language and Literature from the University of Hawaii at Manoa in the United States. In addition, she has a B. A in philosophy from the same university.

My Father and My Two Loves is the first novel published by her in English and translated to other languages and was inspired by the death of her father. In this novel, the author shows the human condition from which we cannot escape such as love, happiness, and death. In the United States, she owns a publishing company and a foundation for victims of earthquakes that occur in Chile and is a professor of English and French literature. She is also working on her next novels, essays, and children's books. Visit her at www. manchesterpublishing.com.

Contents

PROLOGUE

My Father and My Two Loves is a novel by Miryam M. Roche about a daughter and successful psychologist, Victoria Wellington, who thinks her life is perfect in the United States, but when her father dies in Chile, her world collapses with sorrow and despair because she had not seen him for years even though she often called him. Inspired by the psychoanalyst Sigmund Freud, Roche uses dreams to express deep hidden unconscious wishes in which she tries to revive and recreate the past with her father. The author also uses Freud's dreams to develop characters psychologically and to express deep repressed unconscious emotions that we hide from consciousness by different defense mechanisms. For example, in one of the dreams the protagonist, Victoria, dreams that she is in a garden with her father, but when she tries to touch him, he floats and changes and becomes the flowers of the garden. Victoria wakes up frightened and horrified. Then, as the novel unfolds, she gradually has less frightening dreams until she has pleasant ones.

The novel also makes us reflect on existential questions and the meaning of life and how we often do not take into account the love and meaning for our loved ones until a tragedy strikes us with sadness. But amid the sadness, unexpectedly, many of us find love in our lives which helps us to overcome grief and to understand the essence of love and existence. The novel transcends social classes, languages, cultures, and countries because it touches our deepest human nature from which we cannot escape such as love, hope, and death.

The novel is partly an introspective narration of the author's personal experiences and her imagination. Throughout the novel, the author uses her personal experience when she shows beautiful country scenes in huge country style mansions in the South of Chile and Santiago where her upper social class family lives in harmony with the workers. She immortalizes her strong attachment to the traditions that her father both loved and protected. The presence of her father is very strong throughout the novel. Also, the novel portrays the different social classes and socioeconomic stratification in contemporary Chile. For example, the narrator shows a typical country estate in which the speech of the farm workers contrasts with the proper and refined speech of Victoria's rich family. The protagonist's estate mansions contrast with the tall buildings in Santiago. The large country mansions are like a relic of a noble and traditional past. Today, many of them have been converted to rental apartments or have been demolished.

The novel is also anthropological because it shows how the main character adapted to a new culture, but she still held very dear her Chilean cultural traditions such as having large country mansions and love for books and knowledge. She also shows her assimilation and acculturation to the American culture because, for example, she speaks English and lives in an apartment instead of a huge country estate, and holds very dear the American dream. The novel also shows the contrast between traditional values and the destructive forces of contemporary Chilean society. For example, she shows graffiti that reveals despair and frustration on the walls of houses and buildings in downtown Santiago. She also portrays violent student street demonstrations demanding better education and benefits.

The novel is interesting because it shows the disintegration of the Chilean traditional estates in the early years of the last century. The author gives us a tragicomedy of the human condition.

The central themes of the novel are love and death. It is hard to forget the emotional crisis that the protagonist suffers when she learns that her father died and after a while to overcome that trauma, she begins an affair with Pierre that leads her to a love triangle. The author originally thought about writing the novel about her father only, but then she was inspired to include the powerful effect of love to help people overcome and survive grief in the death of a loved one, but she uses the love triangle that one finds in classical medieval romances such as Tristan and Iseut or Lancelot. When the grieving protagonist fills her mind with loving thoughts for her lover, she gradually feels less sad. The love triangle helps Victoria grow and mature emotionally and find true love. The author, in her novel, has the power to awaken feelings in the reader of the sadness, joy, doubt, and jealousy of the characters.

The writer was inspired primarily by her father to write

the novel because he died three years ago and caused her great sadness. Therefore, she needed to express her deep sorrow not only by crying but also writing. She began writing it while traveling by plane across the Pacific Ocean to attend the funeral of her father. By writing, the author not only focused on the sadness, but also on the beautiful moments she shared with her father. Also, the author as a teacher of English and French literature was very inspired by classical writers such as Hemingway, Le Carré, Flaubert, Chateaubriand, Balzac, Sartre, Stendhal, Nerval, and Shakespeare, Cervantes, etc. Also, many South Americans writers such as Borges and Neruda inspired her.

She spent many hours writing her novel in the family home in Santiago and in the country estate and country mansion in Chillán, her penthouse apartment in Hawaii, and other places in the United States.

From a psychological point of view, writing *My Father and My Two Loves* helped the author to express her deep feelings of sadness and reflect on the nature of true love and our human existence.

-Roger Goldberg

PART I

CHAPTER I

One day, early in the summer at sunrise, in Honolulu, Hawaii, the chirping birds woke me up. I smiled with excitement as I saw the sun coming through the large windows of my penthouse in Waikiki. In seconds, I got up happily anticipating a wonderful day, opened the sliding door to the balcony, and looked out across the ocean. I felt the refreshing warm breeze as I watched a yacht sailing towards the horizon. The palm trees in the gardens around the building swayed under the blue sky. Then, I exercised for a while on my treadmill, showered, got dressed, had breakfast, gathered my laptop and bag, and headed for my office where I worked as a psychologist.

When I got into my white Range Rover HSE, I saw that it was eight in the morning and smiled as I heard KTUH University of Hawaii at Manoa radio playing a song I liked very much. That Wednesday, after I came out of the parking lot, I entered into the morning rush hour traffic on Kalakaua

Avenue across the world famous Waikiki Beach. Outside the oceanfront hotels, people were boarding tour buses while others loaded and unloaded luggage. On both sides of the streets, tourists walked excitedly along restaurants and shops in their newly bought colorful aloha shirts, shorts, and slippers. Some tourists were seated on benches under some palm trees in front of the beach while children jumped and laughed as they played in the warm water. I enjoyed filling my mind with wonderful images and thoughts that had powerful effects on my feeling good about my professional success and myself. Besides, that day, I was wearing my favorite beige suit and high heeled beige shoes that made me feel much more confident, successful, and happy. I knew that the way I dressed affected my thinking, feelings, and behavior in a positive way. Ahead, I smelled French fries coming from some fast food outlet and coffee from a Starbucks restaurant. Then, when I saw a jogger along Waikiki beach, I remembered that I had the habit of jogging along Kapiolani Park and Waikiki beach early in the morning on weekends.

Some minutes later, I drove up the edge of Diamond Head cliff. Through the foliage on the right, I saw the blue sea with white splashing waves on the seashore. For a while, I parked at the summit and looked across at the ocean. In minutes, I got out of the vehicle and felt excited when I saw many youths surfing. The soft breeze blew my long blond hair aside. Suddenly, the sun hid behind dark clouds. Thinking it would rain, I rushed to my office. As I drove, I thought about the homework based on cognitive therapy I had assigned to my depressed university student, Peter. I thought that he was still defensive after some sessions to talk about his improper thinking about himself that was affecting his relationship with his girlfriend. But, then I reasoned that he was gradually becoming less defensive because of the homework in which he had to challenge his distorted way of thinking. My goal was to change his beliefs about himself for him to enjoy life. He told me he used to go out with his girlfriend and enjoyed some hobbies, but now he did not feel like doing anything. I had the power to change him to the cheerful university student he used to be.

My destination was on the top floor of a thirty-story office building facing the ocean. The huge pillars at the front entrance reminded me of country style mansions. Even when it rained or was cloudy, I smiled when I arrived at the building and walked through the huge high ceiling lobby to the elevator and my high-heeled shoes clicked on the marble floor. In my office, my secretary, a tall, high cheekbone, tanned skin, with abundant black hair over her shoulders dressed in a flowery local dress, greeted me smiling, "Good morning, Dr. Wellington."

"Good morning, Martha," I said as I walked into my office.

Inside the office, I sat behind my desk and looked around. My office was big and bright. The big cherry wood desk next to a large floor to ceiling sliding door opened to a balcony. The marble floor shined. My chair and the two chairs in front of me were of brown leather. On one of the walls were my diplomas and on another were portraits of some famous psychologists, one of them was Freud. When I opened my laptop, I looked at my schedule where I had the list of the patients for the day. After my first patient, Peter, came in, I offered him coffee or juice.

"Coffee, thank you," he said in a low voice.

I told my secretary to prepare coffee for my patient and me. My secretary quickly went to prepare coffee and was back with the coffee on a tray. As I spoke to my patient about the homework, I took notes. At times, he felt uncomfortable and moved his shoulders nervously when we examined the evidence for and against distorted beliefs. I knew that most depressed patients felt nervous and defensive, so I tried to put him at ease for him to relax. He was practicing new thinking strategies, but he said that it had been difficult to change negative beliefs about himself and the world for positive ones. I had noticed that the cognitive therapy had been effective because at first Peter felt so bad about himself that he did not even take a shower and his eyes looked as if he had not slept for days. But now, he smelled a soft scent of men's cologne, had changed his clothing, and his big green eyes looked at me with curiosity. He had developed a strong bond with me and trusted me, so he seemed to enjoy talking to me. I had faith that the psychologist Beck's cognitive therapy was going to work. I did not want to use psychoanalysis because it would take months or even years to examine the deep causes of his depression that he could have repressed and protected from consciousness by different defense mechanisms. I felt a great sense of accomplishment when I noticed that my therapy was working. Before we finished the session, I assigned him some homework to challenge and encourage him to continue practicing new positive thinking. Then, I smiled at him and said, "You did an excellent job." He smiled back at me. Then, he told me that he had been very busy writing a fifteen-page essay for an English Nineteenth Century Literature course on the romantic poets. I told him that Wordsworth was my favorite poet and he smiled because Wordsworth was also his favorite poet.

While I talked with my patient, my cellular rang, but I did not answer it. Before I saw my next patient, my cellular ran again, but again I did not answer it. As I looked at my agenda for who was my next patient, I wondered who could have been the person who called me with such insistence. I looked at my cellular. It was a call from my younger sister, Yannette, from Chile. I waited for a while to answer. In seconds, I took my cellular and found that my sister had left a message on my voice mail, "Hello sister, our father is very ill. . ." I began to cry with a lot of sadness. Tears streamed down my cheeks like a river. My voice broke when I said, "Dad, I hope that God and the Blessed Virgin Mary help you to regain your health."

After a while, I called my sister. I trembled as I dialed the number.

"Our father is very ill." Yannette said crying.

"What happened?" I asked feeling startled and anxious.

"He is very ill."

"Where do you have him?" I asked.

"In the bed," she said crying.

"Why haven't you taken him to the clinic?" I asked.

My sister paused thinking how to tell me the truth not to hurt me so much, but then she had the strength and said crying and sobbing, "Our father died."

I felt as if the world had crushed on me and I was silent for a long time. Never, never had I felt so much sadness and desperation, but then I was in denial and could not believe it. Then, I cried with deep sorrow. I looked here and there with desperation, but then I had the courage to call my sister.

"Yannette," I said crying, but I almost could not talk.

"Sister, our father died in my arms, his death was very rapid."

"I feel so sad. I cannot believe it," I cried as flashes of images of my father streamed through my mind.

"We felt the same, but our father is dead," she said crying.

I thought that maybe my father had a seizure and was still alive. So I told them to call other doctors.

"Victoria, I know it's hard to accept, but we already have the death certificate," she said crying.

I hung up with despair thinking that my father had probably been presumed dead when perhaps he had a seizure. I was angry with my sister and I would have done anything to go to him and see what had happened, but I did not even have a passport to travel there. I felt very sad and angry thinking about what could have happened. I thought that probably as they were tired with my father being sick, they did not get a second opinion. I cried for a while and then called my sister again and told her to please call in another doctor.

"If you want me to call another doctor to see our father, I will do it," Yannette said reassuring me.

"Yes, please," I said as if I had awakened from a nightmare. Many memories of my father from years ago passed through my mind. I let them continue as they gave me strength. In a flash, many existential questions passed through my mind such as the thought that my father continued existing in the spiritual world and my memory, but not in the physical world. I was one of the youngest of his daughters. My sister Yannette, a lawyer, was the youngest.

Minutes later, I realized that my request for a second doctor to see my father would be useless and not necessary because my father was dead. Then, I thought that my family must have been preparing my father to put him in a coffin. As I reflected, my sister connected me to my sister Carmen.

"Victoria, how are you?" Carmen replied with her broken voice.

"Is it true that our dad died?" I asked shakily.

"Yes, Victoria," my sister cried.

"Is he still warm?" I asked crying.

"Yes."

"Maybe he is still alive"

"No," Carmen said, "The doctor gave his final diagnosis."

"But, please try to revive him giving him mouth to mouth resuscitation so he can revive himself." I said with despair.

"Okay," I heard from Carmen and she went to give him mouth-to-mouth resuscitation.

The line went dead. Trembling, in a state of trance, I walked to the window of my office and opened it. Outside, the sky was covered with dark clouds and it was drizzling. While tears of sorrow rolled down my cheeks, I wondered, "Why didn't you wait a little longer, Dad? Why didn't you let me see you alive for the last time?" While still crying, I thought I should go to Chile as soon as possible.

I told my secretary to cancel all the appointments for the day and for the next two weeks.

Then, quickly, I called several travel agencies to find flights to Chile, but none responded. With despair, I sat on the couch in a state of trance. Then I stood, sighed, and said aloud, "Daddy help me! I have to go to you and see you one last time."

After a few minutes, I quickly left my office. Outside it was raining. I ran through the rain to my Range Rover and then sped to my apartment through the rain.

CHAPTER II

Back in my apartment, I sat behind my desk, turned on the computer, and started searching for information on-line about flights to Chile. Some travel agencies replied, "No flights to Chile." I perspired crying. In other agencies, they asked me if I had a passport. I did not have one! I looked for information about it on the Internet. It was dusk and I still did not have a plane ticket or a passport. In despair, I did not know where to turn for help to get a flight or a passport. All of a sudden, as if a guardian angel had guided me to search the main passport office in Washington, I called there and I never expected that the people there were going to be so humanitarian. As soon as I explained to them my situation, they scheduled an appointment for me the next day at 9:00 in the morning to talk to someone in the Federal Building in Honolulu, where they issued passports. I felt such a relief.

That night, I almost did not sleep at all. As I cried, I felt like calling one of my friends, but instead I thought it was good to mourn. I knew that if I called one of my friends, they would try to stop me from crying. I needed to cry to release my sadness.

At sunrise, when the sun appeared in the horizon, I was still crying. That morning, I took a shower, changed clothing, and headed to the passport office. I did not make up my face because my tears would mess it up. On the way there, I stopped at a photo shop and took a passport picture. In the picture, I looked naive like an adolescent girl, but with swollen eyes.

At the Federal Building, they said I had to fill out a form. I filled it out and gave it to a man behind the counter. The man asked me if I had the flight itinerary.

"I don't have it," I replied.

"We cannot do any processing of passports, if you don't have the itinerary of your trip," the man behind the counter said.

"It's an emergency. My father died and I couldn't find any flights," I pointed out.

"I'm sorry, but I need to see your itinerary," the officer said.

"Yesterday I saw a flight for this evening," I said.

"But what is the itinerary?" he insisted.

"It leaves tonight at 9:20 and arrives in Los Angeles the next morning and then it arrives in Santiago de Chile at 5:29 on Saturday morning."

"The itinerary must come here from the travel agency or the airlines."

"Do you have to see it?" I asked frustrated.

"Yes, and in a printed form," he replied.

"Please see if I can get a passport without a flight itinerary."

"You cannot," he insisted.

"I'll try to find a flight… thank you very much, and can I come back without standing in line again?" I asked anxiously with my eyes swollen from crying.

"Yes, just come to the window without standing in line," he said.

I left the building and called, Walton Bransford, one of my best psychologist friends, to get me a flight to Chile as soon as possible. Walton was working at that time, but he reassured me, "Relax, I'll go to a friend's travel agency and I'll get you a flight!" Without the itinerary, I could not get a passport and travel to my country. The hours passed while waiting for my friend to call me. At about 11:00 a. m., Walton called me to say he had found a flight. The travel agency was going to fax the itinerary to the passport office immediately. I waited for an hour and then entered the office time and again to see if they had sent the fax with the itinerary of the flight.

"Did you receive the itinerary?" I asked the officer anxiously.

"Not yet," the man behind the window replied.

After I asked the officer if he could tell me when I got the itinerary, he said, "Yes." I gave him my name and left the office. I cried as I walked through a high ceiling hallway to a floor to ceiling glass wall. Through the glass, I cried thinking that my family must have been at the wake of my father. Outside, the green grass was scattered with fallen flowers and a light breeze gently moved the palm trees. The sun was beaming and sunshine flooded everything, while tears streamed down my face. I did not even think about my work, but I just wanted to mourn with my family. At times it drizzled. A while later, in desperation, I went back to the office and asked the officer if he had the fax with the itinerary.

"No, Miss," he answered.

"They said they were going to send it immediately," I pointed out.

"But it hasn't arrived yet," he said annoyed.

I left the office and went to look out the window again. The hours passed and I was still not notified. I went back to the office and told another officer, a female, to help me.

"Please help me!" I begged.

"Yes . . . How can I help you?" she asked.

"It's already 1:30 p.m. and my itinerary that they were going to fax here had not arrived yet," I replied anxiously.

The officer asked me my name, "Victoria Wellington," I replied. She wrote it down and went to see if the fax with the itinerary for my flight had arrived. It had not arrived.

"Please. . . Could you please find my flight itinerary online?" I asked.

"It's illegal to do that," she said.

"Please help me!" I asked desperately.

The officer looked at me, "Well. . . I'll try," she said with sympathy.

After a while, she came up with the itinerary that I had anxiously awaited.

"Thank you very much," I said gratefully.

The office was going to close in an hour. She asked me for other information and began to fill the form to complete the information for my passport. For a moment, I left the building while she processed the application. Walking down the hallway, I felt glad to have gotten the itinerary and being able to travel to see my father, but also sad to think that he was on view at the Wake.

Outside the building, standing on the green grass, while waiting for my passport, I called my sister on my cellular.

"Yannette, I got the passport and I'm sure I can travel!" I said with assurance.

"Good!" my sister said.

"I'll arrive on Saturday at 5:20 in the morning."

"But our father will be buried on Friday afternoon."

"Please. . . ask them to wait one more day," I said.

"I will ask and let you know if we can wait for you until Saturday," she said.

"I'll be very happy to see my father for the last time. . . even if it is in the coffin," I said finally.

Without other people noticing, I cried and sobbed discreetly under my sunglasses in the bright sun while walking through the lawn of the Federal Building.

Minutes later, I called my sister again and she told me that they could wait. At times, I could hardly breathe and let my tears fall as my sister told me that my father looked so serene in the coffin while the people prayed.

Finally, in half an hour, I got my passport. I felt calmer, but very sad as I hurried to my Range Rover. I got into my vehicle, left the parking lot, and turned around toward the street where the shopping center was. Then, it began to drizzle and then . . . it rained in torrents. Driving at high speed, I felt despair thinking that my flight was leaving at 9:20 pm. I had to do my shopping for clothes, quickly, for I had no black clothes. I knew my family would be wearing traditional black, so, I had to wear that color.

Soon, I arrived at the shopping center. I bought shoes first, then some black suits and finally Chanel brand handbags. Inside the mall, I heard the bustle of people walking in all directions.

Then, when I left the shopping center, I rushed to my vehicle to get to my apartment. Outside, it was already dark. I called Walton to give me a ride to the airport. As soon as I got back to my apartment, I put the clothing on the living room table and started taking off their tags. As I was doing it, Walton arrived and helped me take them off. He was wearing jeans, a sweater, and sport shoes. He had a British elegance, and we were almost the same age. All of a sudden, when he took a white shirt, a bra was entangled to the button of a shirt. He tried to untangle it, but it seemed to have been sewn to it. I laughed a little embarrassed as I grabbed it and took out the bra. Then, we finished packing the bags. At last, we were ready to go. I was tired and felt hungry, but I did not even have time to eat anything. I did not even change to comfortable clothing because I had to be at the Honolulu Airport an hour and a half before departure at 9:20 that night. It was already eight twenty, so I was very late.

CHAPTER III

In minutes, we rushed to the airport in his green Range Rover HSE. I perspired as we drove through dense night traffic in Waikiki. "Oh, my God," I whispered anxiously as we slowly made our way through the heavy traffic. Walton's face mirrored my anger and frustration. He ran his hands through his hair and said, "We should turn left at the next traffic light to get out of this jam." "Okay, I just want to get to the airport on time," I said desperately. I wished I could get out of the vehicle and run to the other parallel street to get a taxi to the airport. I knew that in one way or another I had to get to Chile. Luckily, we came out of the traffic jam and entered the freeway. Walton drove dangerously over the speed limit in the clear freeway. When we were half-way to the airport, I wished I had called my ex-boyfriend. As we drove in silence, I wished he would not be so controlling and jealous. We had broken our love affair some months ago because he had made a scandal when he saw me talking with just a friend. At first I thought that our romance was going to end like in a fairy tale where the prince and princess live happily ever after, but he became too possessive. Then, I took a deep breath and in tears, I thanked Walton for having helped me. During the drive, my friend tried to comfort me, but I cried all the way to the airport. Tears rolled down my face as I remembered my father happily when I last saw him in the spring sunshine with all the fruit trees blooming in the fresh breeze in the country estate in Chile.

Then, when we were approaching the airport, he reduced the speed and pulled next to the sidewalk and parked along the curb in front of airlines check in. There were crowds of people racing inside the airport to check in their luggage. With tears in my eyes, I quickly got out while my friend took my baggage from the trunk. Then, I took a deep breath again and said good-bye to him. "You'll be all right. Have a nice trip!" he said with a hug.

"Thank you," I said and then ran inside the airport through the crowd with a bag on each side. Inside the airport, as I ran to check in at the American Airlines counter, I heard the loudspeakers announcing the arrivals and departures of flights as tears rolled down my face. In minutes, I checked in. Then, I crossed the security checkpoint and walked into the passenger waiting room to the gate of the plane. At the gate desk, I showed my boarding pass and an agent told me to wait until an airline agent opened the door for boarding. As I waited standing, suddenly, a flash of memories about my ex-boyfriend popped up in my mind. I fought those memories out of my mind, but then, I let the visions continue. I felt a little regret to have broken my romance with him when I missed him and wished he could have been there to hug me, kiss me, and whisper sweet loving words. Then, I wondered, wouldn't it be nice if he were traveling with me. I would tell him to leave everything and go with me. I felt that I loved him and needed to be with him. I was feeling the two extremes of love and grief. In a few minutes, when an airline agent said that the boarding gate was opened, my thoughts directed my attention away from my ex-boyfriend.

Then, as I boarded the plane that was taking me to Los Angeles, I wished I could hear him shouting at me, "I love you, Victoria." I imagined how he would kiss me and sweep me in his arms. Although I longed to be with my ex-boyfriend and throw myself in his arms, I knew that it was better for me to leave behind my thoughts of him. I felt guilty for having thought about my ex-boyfriend when I should have concentrated on mourning my father. I sat in the middle row with a sad and worried face. Tears streamed down my checks. My beige suit made me look paler and my light straight blond hair stood out among the other people with dark hair. Even though my big blue eyes looked sad and swollen from so much crying, I felt glad that I did not miss the flight.

At that time, I did not even notice when the plane took off. Only when it was high in the sky, I realized I was airborne. Often, the flight attendants asked the passengers if we needed anything. I fell asleep sobbing. I woke up when the flight attendants offered food. I had to cover myself with a blanket because it was cold. Then, I continued sleeping and only woke when the plane shook because of turbulences.

The flight to Chile on two airlines was taking about twelve hours. During the flight from Honolulu to California, I slept almost the entire trip. When I awoke, a stewardess began offering food. I did not eat anything. I just wanted to go where my father was as quickly as possible. At four in the morning, the captain announced that the skies were clear in Los Angeles, California and that we would land in about an hour and twenty minutes.

Later, as we approached the airport, I heard the captain say by loudspeaker, "Passengers, your attention please, American Airlines announces the Flight 500 will be landing in to Los Angeles, California, in fifteen minutes. The weather is sunny and with blue skies with 80 degrees temperature. Americans Airlines thank you for having chosen us. Have a wonderful stay in Los Angeles and those of you who are in transit, have a wonderful trip."

Then, the plane prepared to land. After a few minutes, we were flying over Los Angeles International Airport. On board the plane, a flight attendant said over the loudspeaker, "Passengers, please fasten your seatbelt because we're going to land."

In minutes, the plane landed. We arrived at the airport in Los Angeles at 5:20 in the morning as scheduled. I took out my bags, which were in the overhead compartment and the other one that was under my seat. Then, I left the plane. As I walked through the airport lobby, I heard many people speaking in Spanish, English, German, and Japanese.

"What a crowd!" I thought a little confused.

Passengers from around the world walked on either side. While thinking about my father, I went to a restaurant to have a glass of chocolate milk. The plane from Los Angeles to Chile, was taking off at 1:20 in the afternoon, but I had to be at the airport an hour or two before. Time passed very quickly. Around 12:20 p.m. at the Los Angeles International Airport, the airline announced over the loudspeaker, "Passengers, your attention please; Lan Chile announces the departure of Flight 959 to Santiago, Chile."

I walked through a crowd of people to check in at the airlines desk. Then, I went to gate 18 for boarding. There was a group in front of the desk where I had to show my boarding pass. While I waited to weigh my handbags, an airline attendant told me,

"Miss, you can only travel with one bag and a personal effect."

"This is my bag and this is my purse," I replied.

"You must leave a bag. Decide what you carry and what you leave behind?"

"I need my bag and my purse."

"That bag is too big to be a personal effect," the woman said pointing at it.

"Well, all right," I said confused.

In one of the bags were my dark clothes and in the other one was my notebook. After weighing the bags, I said I would leave the bag with the notebook. Fifteen minutes later, the flight assistant approached me again and said,

"I'll let you take them, but if someone has no place to put his or her bags, you'll have to leave one."

"All right, thank you very much," I answered.

I felt frustrated thinking that I had never thought that people at Lan Chile were so strict. I had taken the same bags on the plane in an American Airlines flight, but I never had any problem with them.

In five minutes, I showed my boarding pass and took the shuttle bus to the plane.

As I climbed the steps inside the plane, a tall young

handsome and attractive male stewardess with big brown eyes smiled and greeted me politely.

"Good afternoon, miss, can I help you?"

"Yes, please," I replied, as I passed the bag to him and showed him my seat number.

"Thank you very much," I said.

"It was my pleasure," he replied with a seductive face without knowing I was mourning the death of my father. Men usually found me attractive, but this time I did not care anything else but to get to Chile.

I walked behind him gratefully. A little restless, I sat in a middle row between two persons while the flight attendant put the bag in the compartment above the seat. In a moment, I felt confident that the attendant at the airlines desk would not find me to tell me to leave a bag behind as a checked luggage. Soon, the seat on my right became empty. But then, suddenly, the plane filled up with passengers. I would have wished for the two seats beside me to be empty for me to relax. Before taking off, the captain said, "Passengers, please put your seatbelt on. I wish you a happy journey to Santiago, Chile, with a stop in Lima, Peru."

Since I could not wait to get to Chile, when I heard the word Santiago, Chile, tears started to run down my cheeks. The trip was taking about seven hours. Later, the flight attendants began to distribute food to the passengers in their carts. The classic tall and slim stewardesses of Lan Chile had an imposing beauty and elegance. They looked very young, beautiful, and elegant with their caps and uniforms. Some of the female stewardesses had baby faces, rolled their black, brown, or blond hair under their caps, and held their heads very high. I remembered that many Chilean adolescents wanted to be stewardesses. The classical music that was playing in the background made me feel more sadness and despair. I cried desperately as I thought that I could only see my father through the window of the coffin. After a while, I was served a snack of cake with peach jelly. The food was good. The Coca-Cola was very refreshing. Sometimes, the attractive young male stewardess who helped me with my bags earlier looked and smiled at me. I pretended that I did not notice it. I was not in the mood of being seduced. I did not want anyone to see me mourn. I never thought I would feel this deep sadness, I thought as I ate.

I felt my hopes and dreams had collapsed with the death of my father. But I thought that my father, from heaven, would give me strength to become a famous writer. After I ate, as the plane crossed the Pacific Ocean, I started writing my emotions to express my deep sorrow for my father. My mind was occupied with his memory when I said, "I write this novel in honor of my father and like Shakespeare, I would like to adapt it to a play and a movie." After a while I looked around. Some people talked among themselves while others watched movies on the screens in front of them. Others listened to music. Suddenly, the hostess came offering Coca-Cola, water, or wine. An hour later, we were served dinner. The roast chicken, mashed potatoes, tossed greens, and cake for dessert looked delicious, but I had no appetite.

"Red wine, please," I asked one the stewardesses.

"Sure," the stewardess said.

Soon, I took a few sips of wine. Then, I drank the large glass dry. I had not had any wine for a long time. I felt dizzy, but I did it on purpose because I wanted to fall asleep.

Hours later, I woke up and looked around. There was

silence on the plane. Occasionally, I heard some people walking down the aisle to the bathroom.

Then the pilot said, "The plane will make a stop of one hour, in Lima, so we recommend that the passengers do not get out of the plane."

I began to feel cold as we approached Lima. Within minutes, the plane was landing at the airport there.

During the stopover, I could not contain my tears. Some people left while others boarded the plane. An hour later, we took off for Santiago. Thinking about the novel I had started writing about my father, I wondered if I should write it in the present or past tense. The past tense made me feel as if I was not suffering from the death of my father. How would it be to write it in the present tense? I thought my spirit cried like a storm with thunder and lightning.

Two hours before the plane landed in Santiago, I opened a bag beneath my seat, pulled out a black jacket, black pants, and white shoes. In the bathroom, I changed my clothes and then returned to my seat. While making an effort not to cry, the more I cried.

CHAPTER IV

It was very cold that Saturday morning at 5:20 when the plane landed in Santiago International Airport. Sad with tears in my eyes, I turned my face toward the window and saw lights like stars amidst the misty fog. Then, I made my way through the crowd and walked out of the plane quickly. I went to Immigration to show my passport and get a tourist visa. After that, I went to get my bags and as I walked shivering with cold and sadness, I breathed deeply trying not to cry so much. I came out and saw a crowd of people outside of Customs. It took me some time to recognize my mother and my sister because they looked very different after all these years. Suddenly our eyes met, I dropped my bags and I ran to embrace my mother and my younger sister Yannette. "Daughter, your father," my mom embraced me crying and I hugged her crying too, while my sister cried at her side to share our grief. My mother and sister looked very sad with their long black coats and black boots. With sadness I looked at my mother, who was tall, blonde, with bright blue eyes, but at that time they looked puffy from mourning. I never thought that I would see them so sad. I wanted to cry loudly, but with great effort I tried to hold back my tears. I regretted to have been abroad for such a long time.

After we greeted, we walked outside the airport and then headed to my sister's Range Rover. It was painfully cold that morning. I noticed that my mother was much thinner than when I had gone to the United States. As we walked to the vehicle, we talked.

In the Range Rover, my sister put on the heat and we continued talking. The three of us had swollen eyes from so much crying.

"Daughter, your father must be very pleased with your coming," my mother said.

"Yes mom, as a daughter it was my duty to be here," I said.

Then, my mom looked at me in silence as tears streamed down her cheeks.

"Thank God that they could wait another day," I said.

"Yes . . . we had to wait for you," Yannette replied as tears streamed down her cheeks.

For a while, the three of us shed tears, and then we continued talking. As we drove through downtown Santiago, the Range Rover entered some narrow streets. The houses on both sides of the street had walls with graffiti. We smelled smoke coming through the chimneys of some houses. Later, the fog looked like smoke when the Range Rover entered wider streets. It was beginning to clear at dawn. At times, the windows were moist with condensation in the morning. Meanwhile, I looked at the big houses that were on both sides of the street. Then, we drove through a main avenue in Las Condes. Shortly afterwards, we passed a few houses with large gardens. Ahead, when we finally turned the Range Rover to our family mansion and drove through an iron gate, I shivered with sadness as we went up the driveway with tall trees on both sides. And then for the first time after many years, I saw the tall pillars of the family mansion. We could see the chandeliers in some rooms that had the curtains drawn open. There was the huge family mansion. It looked as I remembered it. The tall trees still had some autumn leaves. I saw many cars around the driveway and the backyard and that made me sadder because I knew why they were there. We parked in front of the house next to the garden. There was a worker who ran to greet us. We got out of the vehicle and our German shepherd, Max, ran to greet us wagging his tail and then brushed against us. I could feel Max's soft fur. The house was quiet that morning. Then, the big front door of the house opened and I was surprised when I saw a girl with pale skin, white like snow, long blonde hair, blue eyes, and about twelve years old.

"My daughter, Katherine whom we call Katy," Yannette said with tears in her eyes.

"Hello, Auntie," my niece said running to greet me with a gracious face, but with swollen eyes. I hugged her crying.

I imagined that my nieces were shorter, but Katy was very tall.

It was still early and everyone was in bed. We walked straight to the bedrooms where my nephews, nieces, sisters, and brothers were sleeping. First, we went to my sisters' bedrooms. Sadly, with very sad faces crying, we embraced. My brothers woke up upon hearing us crying. Then, we went to their bedrooms. We hugged crying without saying a word.

After we talked for a while, I continued greeting my other relatives.

When I went to another bedroom, I saw some adolescent girls who sat on the bed.

"Who are they?" I asked Yannette.

"She is Jocelyn and we call her Yosi. My youngest daughter and she is Leslie. Marlenne's daughter, our cousin," Yannette said.

Crying we hugged and kissed. Yosi had tan skin, so she was not pale as Katherine, but like her grandfather, she had a turned-up nose.

Then, we went to another bedroom.

"Marlenne," Yannette said.

We hugged each other while crying. I had not recognized her. She was a little fat and looked more mature, but as pale as we were. I knew she had married a wealthy owner of a bakery and had two daughters, Leslie and Pamela, who were very smart. Pamela was receiving a social worker degree from the University of Chile. Then, I went to the other bedrooms. I spent some time greeting my relatives. The house with about thirty rooms was filled with family. Later, my mother told me that the whole family would meet in the chapel at Park of the Remembrance, at nine o'clock. After we talked for a while, I went to bed. In bed, I could not sleep thinking about memories of my father. Then, thinking about my father, I fell asleep. A while later, with the noise of conversations that was coming through the bedroom door that was ajar, I woke up. I looked at my cell phone and saw that it was eight o'clock. I got up, showered, and changed clothes. In the dining room and living room and around the house, were many family members who had come and kept coming to go to the chapel where my father was. Some cried while others talked. Some ladies who knew the rosary were praying in the chapel.

CHAPTER V

At **nine in** the morning, my family, relatives, and our friends got together in grief to go to see my father for the last time. That day, my sister, Yannette, drove her Range Rover. In it, some of my brothers, sisters, and my mom went to the Memorial Park. Silently, I felt my tears running down my face. We all knew that day would be the last time we would see him. We were torn with grief.

When we arrived at the Memorial Park, we saw an imposing very high, solid iron gate. Upon entering through the gate, we saw beautiful patches of flowers and tall trees in the gardens and lawns. We drove around a garden and then at last we stopped the vehicle and parked. Crying we got out of the vehicle and then walked towards the chapel under some high ceiling corridors with granite floor. There was classical music by Bach playing in the background. The music made me feel sadder. Before entering the chapel, I heard that some of my family and friends were praying. The chapel's door was open. Crying, I saw that my father's coffin was covered with beautiful flowers such as roses, jasmines, pansies, daisies, etc. His family and friends were gathered around him. It was brown, with the photo of Pope John Paul II on it. Crying, I looked at my father through the glass of the coffin. His face looked very clean and without any wrinkles. As tears rolled down my face, I felt desperation and deep sadness.

"Before you came, your father had a tear in his right eye," my mother said crying.

"But now, he doesn't have it," I said as I looked at him and found him so thin and different as I had last seen him.

"Yes, daughter," my mom replied.

"I think it was the tear that made it possible for me to come," I said.

"Your father must be happy you're here," my mother said.

I kissed the glass above his face and said, "Dad, I love you very, very much and thank you very much for letting me see you again."

Standing, my closest relatives and friends held hands praying the rosary around my father. Then, we sat around him. Inside and outside, the chapel was filled with family and friends in dark mourning clothes. I also wore a black suit. Many relatives and friends came to hug me and give me their condolences. One of the youths approached me.

"Don't you know me?" he asked.

I looked at him and then I recognized that he was one of my nephews who were little boys when I went abroad. Now, they were very tall. Some of my nephews were dressed in uniforms of the armed forces. Sometimes we prayed. I suggested my family and friends to talk about unforgettable anecdotes or experiences with my father. From heaven, my father must have listened to them. One referred to what happened to him once in his country estate mansion, when my father was lying in the shade of a tree and a calf came up to him. Gradually, this animal took the handkerchief from his pocket and ran across the meadow and ate it.

Later, we prayed again. At four in the afternoon, we took our father for burial in the holy courtyard of the Memorial Park, which is the most prestigious in Chile. They put our father on a cart and brought him slowly to the place of his burial, as we walked behind him. Minutes later we reached the place. They had placed an awning, lots of flowers, and several seats. My father was placed on many flowers. The most immediate family members sat in front of him. We prayed and then heard the song "My Dear Old," by Leo Dan, which was his favorite song. Then, we stood to hear a speech by the eldest grandson, who was spoiled by my father.

Family and friends wept as we listened to the speech. Before lowering the coffin, a priest blessed him with holy water and we prayed and looked at him one last time. Crying, we looked at the body of our father, slowly lowered down covered with flowers to the paradise of our Lord Jesus Christ. Embraced we comforted one another asking our Lord Jesus Christ to receive him with open arms and at peace.

After we buried our father, we walked in silence back to the parking lot, got into the vehicle, and left the Memorial Park with a deep sense of loss and sadness. From the outside, we cried as we looked at the place where my father was.

"He is in a place with many trees and flowers . . . as his farm," my mother said sobbing.

CHAPTER VI

The next day at dawn, amid the gloom and cold, I went to the second floor of the mansion and from the balcony of the library I looked at the garden thinking about my father. The sky was pale, but then it changed in color as I said to myself that now nothing would be the same without my father. I felt nostalgic, thinking that I no longer would hear his interesting conversations. That morning, it was difficult to describe my emotions as I looked back through my memory. My father was a doctor and loved his farm. He was the eldest of two brothers. As a child he had a nanny who spoke Spanish and British English. In the summers, his parents often traveled to England and France with him and his sister. Both of them had a European look with very fair skin and blue eyes. They still had relatives there. My father and his sister spoke English with a British accent. When he was seventeen, my father went to the Catholic University to study medicine. He studied there for a while and then switched careers. He liked to study psychology and continued studying that. With his friendly personality, he endeared himself to all his fellow students. He had charisma and was a great conversationalist. My father attracted people to him. The women fell in love with him easily. After a year, he returned to medical studies and graduated as a doctor. For a time, he practiced medicine, but then joined the military school.

In the summer of 1945 when he was an army officer, my father met my mother at a gala at the military school. He wore his uniform. Women found him charming and looked at him, but he fell in love with my mother at first glance.

She was a light-skinned woman who was studying in a normal school to be a teacher of English literature. He did not continue with the military. He left and married my mother thinking he was going to work as a doctor.

They moved to a large mansion at the country estate of her family in the south of Chile. The following year, days before Christmas, Magaly, their first daughter was born. The next year, Carmen was born. Both were very blonde and had blue eyes. After that, Hugo was born, then me, then my sister Yannette and then, my brother Roberto.

My parents had told me they had nannies and several maids to take care of the children and things around the house. So when we were children, many times, my dad and mom took us out for a walk around the garden. The nannies helped them with the children while the maids cooked and cleaned the house. After some years, the oldest daughter got married and in that year had her first child. My father was very happy with his grandson. With him, he wandered around the farm. The grandson was blonde like his parents and grandparents. My sister and her husband were doctors.

Sometimes they left their son with my parents. The next year, my sister had a daughter, who was blonde and had blue eyes. From time to time, my sister and my brother-in-law also left their daughter at my parent's house. A year later, another son was born. He, like his sister, grew up closer to his parents than his grandparents.

Magaly and her husband continued the tradition of having maids who wore uniforms. My sister Magaly invited her parents to heated pools and spas at country resorts. My dad and my mom enjoyed them with their grandchildren. Occasionally, the kids wanted to get into the pool at the house, but it was not heated in the fall and winter. My parents loved going with their daughter, son-in-law, and grandchildren to the cabins that had heated pools in winter. My sister's children seemed to be British. They were tall and very blond. Some of them had gotten university degrees at a very early age, like the rest of the family. At home, from a very early age, we were encouraged to learn. That inspired me to study cognitive psychology, specializing in learning, at the University of Cambridge. When I was in the United States and in England, my family insisted that I return to Chile.

"Victoria, when are you coming home to your country?" My parents used to ask me when talking on the phone.

"When I get my doctorate in psychology and English literature," I used to say.

So in that way, time passed, studying at the university and getting many degrees. The more I succeeded in my studies, the more degrees I wanted to get. Then not only I wanted to get many degrees, but I also wanted to build a prestigious university like Cambridge. For that goal, I wrote many novels. I knew that I would make money publishing them. I had written some in Spanish, and others in English, German, and French. Famous writers such as Hemingway, Fitzgerald, Wordsworth, Shakespeare, Le Carré, Flaubert, Chateaubriand, Balzac, Nerval, Jean de Meun, Thomas Moore, had inspired me. I had written some novels from a psychological and sociological perspective. I almost never took vacations. I spent all my time studying, working, and writing. I refused to travel to my country, without having succeeded in everything. I had achieved almost everything: my studies, profession, and my novels. I was thinking of publishing the novels in the spring when it was autumn in Chile, but I could not resist going home when my father died. I felt that everything I had obtained was not important as the life of my father.

"I should have come to Chile when he was still alive. My daughter came to say farewell, my father must have thought when he saw me crying," I thought.

The day that I heard of the death of my father, I did not care about titles, novels, or material things, I just wanted to be near my family. The change was abrupt and I felt depressed as reflected by Van Gogh in his painting "The Starry Night," in which the world is changed into a hurricane.

That morning, after thinking about my father, I had breakfast with my family and friends. In the afternoon, we gathered in the dining room and ate silently because we felt my father's absence. Through the large windows, we saw the mist that looked like smoke. It was drizzling.

That day we went to bed early. While sleeping, I dreamt I saw my father walking in a garden. He walked among roses, jasmines, carnations, and camellias. He smiled when the flowers tickled his face. It was spring. The buds of the flowers grew and quickly turned into flowers. When I tried to approach him, my father rose floating in the air. His body was covered with flowers. I ran through the garden while he floated around trees and vines hanging from the balconies. Then he was transformed into flowers and then he returned to be as he was before. I woke up crying. For a while, I thought about the dream. Fragmented memories of it made me think about the meaning of existence. My father was in the world of pure ideas and thoughts, which reminded me of the philosophical ideas of Plato and Descartes. Then, thinking of the dream, I remembered a poem by Gerard de Nerval, in which a ghost is transformed into flowers and then becomes the garden as in my dream. I fell asleep again.

The next day I woke up early and stayed in bed thinking about my father. At times, I heard conversations and footsteps in the hallway as I looked at the portraits and country scenes that hung on the white walls. I got up at about ten o'clock that morning. My bedroom was on the second floor. There was a queen-sized bed that had a pink sheet covered with blankets of wool from our sheep in the farm. Through the window, I saw that it was a beautiful day, but it was a little cold.

After breakfast with the rest of my family and some friends, we walked to the backyard, which was our favorite place. Outside, the trees had already lost some of their yellowish brown leaves that blew across the courtyard. The leaves crackled like paper because it had not rained.

As we walked through the courtyard, we looked at the workers sweeping the leaves.

"Good morning," one of them told us, putting the rake on the side.

"Good morning, good job!" some of us said.

"Thank you, miss," he replied.

We continued walking.

"What happened to the apple tree that was here?" I asked with curiosity.

"It was cut down," my older brother Hugo said.

That day we had lunch at about one p.m. on the dining room of the first floor. The maids had already set the table with a white tablecloth. Two silver candlesticks matched the silverware for each of us. It also had white plates with cloth napkins. The breadbaskets, wine, and salads could not be absent from the traditional lunch of my family. Talking we sat around a rectangular table. Then, maids began to serve lunch, which was chicken soup with peas from which steam rose up, filet mignon, and strawberries for dessert. Classical music was playing very softly in the background. My mother kept the tradition of serving the meal to everyone and not passing the plates from hand to hand. That day the fireplace warmed the dining room.

"It seems like spring," my mom said as we ate and the sun poured through the large window.

"Yes," one of my brothers said.

"It has to be the San Juan summer," my mother said thinking about a few hot days in winter.

"Here the weather is warmer than in the south," Yannette said.

While listening to the rattling of the dishes and conversations, I thought that Yungay was very cold and icy at the time.

"Victoria for how long are you going to be here?" I asked my brother Hugo, who was very optimistic.

"I'll be here for two weeks," I said.

"It cannot be," Hugo said.

"Yes, I have to go back for my work."

"Stay longer!" Roberto said, who was tall, pale, and blond, with big blue eyes.

"Besides my work, I want to publish other novels," I told them.

"Why not publish here?" Yannette, who was very sensitive and cried easily, said.

"Yes, Victoria," my mother said.

As we ate and talked, we finally decided that I would stay a little longer. In that way, we could go skiing in Portillo on weekends.

CHAPTER VII

I spent that week with my family and friends. On Wednesday of the following week, the chirping birds and the crickets woke me up at sunrise. For a while, I thought about my father. The more I thought about him, the more I was inspired to continue writing the novel that I had begun on the plane crossing the Pacific Ocean. I got up, I went to the library, and sat behind the desk where my manuscript was. It was the first day that I wrote the new chapters of my novel in my parents' house. I wondered about a lot of existential questions while writing. Here was where my parents taught me to walk and where I grew up. I thought of the past. Occasionally, you could hear the conversations of the workers around the house.

After a while, I wrote several chapters for the novel. Then, I looked at the garden through a large window that opened to a balcony. Outside, there were still white and pink roses swaying in the autumn breeze. Beyond the garden, some tree leaves fell and blew across the tennis court. The thrushes were chirping and hopping on the branches of the rose bushes.

"How beautiful is the country!" I thought.

The garden had a fountain in the middle. That day, the sparkling water in the fountain splashed around in the garden. Sometime later, one of the workers began to remove the leaves from the pool. He had not realized that I was on the balcony.

"Aren't the leaves floating in the pool beautiful?" I said.

"Yes, just as you are, Miss!" the worker said graciously.

After breakfast with the rest of my family, we went for a walk. I had forgotten how cold autumn days could be in Chile. Therefore, I did not bring the right clothing. That morning Yannette lent me a jacket. For a while, we walked around the garden.

"This fall has been very cold," Yannette said.

"I never thought it was going to be so cold," I said.

My sister Yannette had a little white dog called Niki playing near me while I petted him. Sometimes, I jumped frightened when the dog opened its mouth to bite me. But my sister told me that the dog did not bite but was just playful. Then the dog went away, and we arrived at the garden. When we had walked and talked for a while, the teenage daughters of Yannette, Yosi and Katy, arrived.

"Mom, can you give us permission to get together with some friends?" asked Yosi, who was very studious, loved dogs and children, and wanted to study to become a pediatrician.

Yannette was angry to hear that. Although her youngest daughter was spoiled, Yannette was very strict with the girls. No doubt my sister protected her children because she wanted them to grow up well.

Yosi insisted that she gave her permission, but my sister said she would not with people she did not know.

"You're very selfish, mom," Yosi said furiously.

Then Yosi began to cry and walked quickly towards the house. My mother saw her crying and asked what was wrong. Yosi told her that Yannette had not given her permission. My mom wanted to give her permission, but then thought it would upset Yannette. My mom told my niece that Yannette had not given permission to protect her from bad friends. Yosi understood and went to the library to read a book.

My sister told me that her two daughters were fascinated with their studies and excelled with good grades. My sister had motivated my nieces to be very studious and generous since a very early age.

That day my sister told me that her daughters made her nervous when she did not give them permission to go out with friends. .

"I love my daughters, but they feel very misunderstood because I do not allow them to go out with friends," Yannette said worriedly.

"Adolescent girls become very rebellious because they're in a period of cognitive, social, and emotional development between childhood and adulthood," I said.

As a psychologist, I told my sister that all parents went through similar situations with their adolescents.

"Sometimes I buy them clothing, but they never put them on," Yannette said.

"Other parents say similar things about their adolescents," I said.

My sister, Yannette, felt more relaxed after we talked.

Then my mother came, who was blond like us and cared

a lot for her garden. She sang as she watched her flowers or planted seeds. She loved nature.

"Daughters, today we will trim the roses," my mother said. She told me her rosebushes had been very good this year. There were still some roses left. Then, my mom gave us chocolates.

"These chocolates are very delicious!" I said.

"We bought them in France," my mom said.

My mother had gone to Lourdes shrine in France to pray for the health of my father. She told me that she had visited the palace of Louis XIV and was fascinated with the extravagance of the palace with its gardens and bedroom walls of gold. Then, she told us that they had also visited Buckingham Palace in London when she got married.

Then, my brother Robert, who was fought over by women, came. He was smart, intelligent, handsome, and a very good person. But he was more concerned with the country estate of my parents than women. We said he had to marry soon and not remain a bachelor. He liked intellectual women who did not just worry about clothing and makeup.

Then, we went to the tennis court. The road was slippery. The day before, in the afternoon, it had rained. Later, as we returned to the house, the door opened and a maid came out. She was going to tell us that lunch was ready.

Inside the house, we sat down at the table to have dinner. That day the fireplace warmed the dining room. On the table, there was a white embroidered tablecloth, a breadbasket with bread, and bottles of red wine. There was still at home, the custom of serving the food to each person. In other families, they placed the roast in large platters and each took on his plate as much as he wished to eat. My father had a passion for tradition. As we talked, the maids served us dinner.

That day, Mom had ordered chicken soup with peas, roast beef, salad with spinach and tomatoes, and peaches with chocolate and nuts for dessert. As before, we always ate healthy meals. Proteins were very important. My mother told us that the food was to nurture us and not only to enjoy its taste. During the meal we remembered my father.

"You should have come when our father was well," my sister Magaly said.

"Yes," I replied a little guilty.

"You were ungrateful for not having visited your parents for such a long time," Magaly said angrily.

"Victoria must have been very busy that is why she didn't come before," my Mom said, not wanting to see her children in discord.

"Yes, you're right, I felt guilty for not coming sooner," I was almost in tears as I thought I was one of his youngest daughters and maybe my absence had caused his death.

"I think my father would have lasted a little longer if he had been treated better," I said.

"How can you say that Victoria when you didn't come to see him for years," Yannette said tearfully.

"I'm sorry," I said.

"My father had nurses, but I diapered him with my own hands," Yannette said crying.

Tears rolled down my cheeks, not knowing that my father was so ill.

"Children, your father is now in the high heaven of our Lord and therefore wants his children to be united and not fight," my mother said trying to preserve harmony in the family.

Then, one by one, we rose from the table and went for a walk around the house. As we walked, the dogs wagged their tails. I remembered stories of my childhood. They made me feel happy and sad. I felt the two extremes of emotions as I looked and talked. The house was as big as I remembered. The sounds of the fall season were the same. For a while, I remembered the green fields around the house in springtime. Then, I thought of the harvesting season.

The house was pretty much as before. One change I noticed was that they had planted more trees. A few peach trees that my father had planted still had some fruits on them. All the trees were taller. As we walked, we remembered our childhood with our father.

"Victoria, do you remember when you climbed that cherry tree?" my mother said looking at the tree.

"Yes, of course," I smiled.

There were still some cherries. One of the workers climbed to get some. It was customary for children to eat the fruit perched on the fruit trees.

"Dad took good care of his peach trees," Yannette said.

"Yes! He did. He planted this peach tree orchard," said Roberto, who loved nature as much as the romantic poets.

My dad seemed to be swaying the branches of the peach trees.

"Victoria, I planted many peach trees," I remembered having heard my father, one of the last times I talked with him by phone.

"Your dad felt happy when he imagined that you and your children, speaking English, would eat his peaches," Mom said smiling.

"It would be wonderful if you had a *gringuito* or *gringuita*, my dad told me in one of the many times we talked on the phone," I said.

My father felt very happy when I said, "Yes, dad, I'll have *gringuitos*."

Our dog, Max, ran around wagging his tail and from time to time jumped on us.

"Your father wanted to see all his children with their own children," my mother said.

"My father was very loving with his grandchildren," Yannette said.

"Your father will help you from the high heaven of our Lord Jesus Christ for you to have your own children, Victoria," my mother said.

"I hope God and the Virgin Mary make that wish come true," I replied.

During that week, after writing several hours in the morning, I had breakfast with the rest of my family. Then, I continued writing. My goal was to write the novel and publish it in Chile. Sometimes, I let the cold inspire me as Hemingway had done in his best novels. Other times, I lit the fireplace.

CHAPTER VIII

One morning that week over breakfast, Karen, my niece, Magaly's daughter, who was tall, had long blond hair and blue eyes arrived with her two children. Monserrat, who was six years old, was called Monchi and Matías, who was seven years old, was called Mati.

"My granddaughter with her children," my mother said, standing from the table to greet them as she looked at them from the open window. I still called my niece Karen, Karincita, because she was just a little girl when I left for the United States.

The children ran to greet my mom with a hug and kiss.

"Say hello to your aunt Victoria," mother said to her great-grandchildren.

"Hi, auntie Victoria," the children said, hugging me.

"Hi, Monchi and Mati, how are you?" I replied affectionately.

At home, we were concerned that all the children spoke

English. Their grandfather, a doctor, bought them many English books and encouraged them to speak English.

We had breakfast together. Then we went for a walk around the house. We walked by the side of tall trees surrounding the garden. Some birds flew out of the bushes when they heard us coming. We smiled when we heard a child of a worker who whistled very harmoniously imitating the song of a thrush.

"These children know very well the bird's behavior," I said.

"Yes," Karincita replied.

The dogs ran around us whining while we talked.

We walked to the garden. There, we sat on a green bench as we talked and watched the children play and laugh around us. Monchi and her older brother Mati laughed as they chased after their little poodle that hid in the tall rosebushes. After they grabbed him, Monchi climbed a cherry tree while Mati held the dog. Then, the children ran around the rosebushes while the dog jumped and whined next to them.

"Look Mati!" Monchi shouted happily as she pointed at something on a rosebush.

"What?" Mati replied with curiosity.

"That nest," Monchi said pointing at it. Mati ran with curiosity to look at the eggs.

"No darling, don't take them out," Karincita said stopping them from doing it. The children ran to her side and she kissed them. Monchi and Mati continued playing, laughing, and shouting in the garden. Then, they cut carnations to compete with who had more. After that, the two children sat on the green grass that was dotted with some leaves. Then, they placed carnations in rows on the grass and asked each other questions.

"How many flowers are there?" Monchi asked Mati showing him her row with carnations.

"Five," Mati shouted.

"Good," Monchi praised her brother and clapped her hands.

Mati felt very happy.

"Now, you ask me questions," Monchi said.

The children were having a lot of fun while we looked at them happily. As the children counted the flowers, the dog got down on his belly and watched them attentively.

My father had taught them the logic of reasoning, the inverse relation between addition and subtraction. Sometimes my father used chocolates to show the inverse relationship $(a + b - b = a)$.

"How many flowers are there now?" Mati asked when he added five.

"Ten," Monchi said shouting cheerfully.

Then, they cut different flowers and placed them in rows while their dog ran after them wagging his tail. Sometimes, the children threw some flowers to the dog and the dog ran after them and brought them back to their feet.

"How many flowers are of the same color?" Monchi asked, when she added one pink pansy to the four white carnations.

"Four carnations,"

"How many are now the same color?" Monchi asked when she added six white carnations.

"Ten."

Monchi jumped and screamed with delight and gave Mati a kiss on the cheek when he knew the answer. Other times, she clapped and said, "Excellent Mati!" Monchi had learned from the adults to reinforce good behavior.

"I remember that Dad taught us to understand arithmetic, showing us and seeing changes," I said.

"In this garden we learned the essence of the logic of mathematical reasoning," Yannette said.

Looking at the trees, we remembered how our father taught us how to measure without numbers.

"Which tree is the tallest? Or, which tree is taller? Our father used to ask us," Yannette said.

"Do you remember when the cows were grazing in groups in the farm and our father used to ask us which group had more cows?" I said.

"Your father encouraged you to develop your quantitative reasoning skills while I encouraged you reading skills," my mom said.

When our father realized that we knew how to compare quantities without numbers, he then taught us to count with number. We remembered all the fun when he taught us the correspondence between one and many; for example, he used to tell us to make us think. "If there are three vases, each with four carnations, how many are there altogether?" When we did not know the answer, he said to us to place the vases in a row and the flowers on each vase to find the answer.

As we continued walking and looking at the garden wall covered with vines and dotted with flowers, I remembered that as a child I had written the commutative and associative properties of addition and multiplication there. With curiosity, I stood and walked across to the garden wall.

"There is still what I wrote a long time ago," I said smiling as I lifted the vines with flowers and looked under it.

"What?" my mother said smiling with curiosity.

I showed her what I had written on the wall.

As the fence of the garden was almost always covered with vines, they had not noticed it.

"How interesting! As it was underneath the ivy, I hadn't noticed it," my mom said surprised.

Monchi and Mati ran next to us shouting happily to see what we were looking at.

"(a + b) = (b + a)" Monchi read.

"What does it mean?" I asked.

"It's the commutative property of addition," Monchi said.

"Bravo!" we applauded.

Mati continued to read eagerly what I had written on the fence of the garden.

"It's the associative property of addition (a + (b + c) = (a + b) + c)," Mati shouted with joy when he looked under the vines.

Then, I asked them if they understood other properties.

"What property is this, a + b - b = a?" I asked.

"It's the property of inverse relationship between addition and subtraction," Mati said jumping and feeling successful.

"Excellent!" I congratulated him with a hug.

Next, we continued wandering around. After we left the garden, we walked through bamboos that were on the side of the tennis court. The bamboo leaves tickled our faces when they brushed against us. At that time, there were many fallen leaves on the ground. The children ran beside us playing. Suddenly, one of them asked, "Where is our poodle?"

The children ran together to get their dog that had ran away. Monchi held and petted her dog while Mati jumped next to her.

The birds perched and preened around the fountain in

the garden. It had figures of dolphins and out of their mouths water was spouting. At that time, the fountain was covered with green algae with the change of climate.

"The two children are in the preoperational period of cognitive development ranging from two years to seven years, but they knew how to reason as if they were in the fourth stage of development," I said.

"I started to stimulate them intellectually since they were born because I often read to them and had developmental toys," Karincita said.

"How interesting! Children acquire their first schemes of knowledge through their actions and reflexes at first and still they benefit intellectually when parents read to them," I said.

I explained that children's early schemes or knowledge structures were the basis for acquiring new knowledge.

"Aunt, you know that I love child developmental psychology."

"You should study it."

"Yes, next semester I want to resume my studies."

As we talked, we smelled *empanadas*. Then, a worker came with a basket. He brought us freshly made *empanadas*. It was a pleasant surprise.

"Good afternoon, how are the misses doing?" he said as he approached us.

"Enjoying our walk, thanks," we said. "What did you bring us?"

"One of your favorite foods," he replied taking meat pies wrapped in napkins.

"Thank you very much!" we answered in chorus.

We opened the napkins and started eating.

"Mmm, they're delicious," Karincita said.

I liked the *empanadas* very much, but I had the habit of taking out the onions because I liked the delicious moist inside of the crust. Some of my brothers and sisters remembered our childhood and giggled when they saw me take the onions out of the *empanadas* and put them in the napkins.

The children were still counting flowers on the grass, but they took a break to eat meat pies. As they ate, the juice from the pies ran down the sleeves of their pullovers, but a maid cleaned them.

"Darlings, eat carefully," Karincita said to her children.

"Yes, Mom," they answered.

Then, we continued the conversation.

"Piaget is a little rigid in his theory of children's cognitive development," Karincita said.

"Yes, a little."

"Auntie, what are the four periods of child cognitive development according to Piaget?"

"The sensory from birth to two years, the preoperational from two years to seven, the concrete from seven to eleven and the formal period from eleven to fifteen years."

"So, my children are in the preoperational period."

"Yes."

"I thought they were in the formal stage of development."

"That period comes after, according to Piaget."

"But my children know how to reason."

"That's why Piaget's theory is controversial."

After we ate *empanadas*, the children went back to play. We continued talking. That day the breeze was warm.

"In the concrete period, do children have the ability to classify objects?" Karincita asked.

"Yes, but objects that are present," I said.

"Then on the next stage, children can reason about things that are not present?"

"That's right."

"Many cognitive-experimental studies with children have indicated that children can reason much earlier than Piaget says."

"It's good to stimulate children cognitively."

"Yes, of course, in that way, they learn to reason and develop their ability to learn."

After a while, we kept walking and talking. Later, we stopped for a while in the vegetable garden. There were still some tomatoes.

"Shall we get some?" I asked.

"Yes, of course," my mother said.

The children picked tomatoes and continued to compete between each other, who could count the best. On dry leaves, they put the tomatoes in rows. Monchi covered them with her pink sweater when she subtracted and took out her sweater when she added. The children loved to learn, playing.

The warm breeze shook the foliage of the tall trees. When it began to drizzle, we went back to the house. Karincita's husband, a Navy Captain, had already arrived.

We had lunch together. Through the window, the sun shone and it was no longer raining. In the afternoon, we picked up my sister's daughters at the Mary Immaculate Conception School. In front of the school, we saw Kati and Yossi chatting with friends. When I saw my nieces, I thought that like their mother they distinguished themselves with their light skin, green eyes, and blond hair. My niece's cheeks were pink as they ran toward us. I thought that I must have looked like them when I went to school with Yannette, who was two years younger than me. They also had learned well the essence of the logic of arithmetic reasoning.

Then, we went for a walk. As we walked towards the pool, I noticed that there were still bushes with berries. Besides the pool, we sat in lounge chairs that were covered with blue and white striped cushions. That day, the sun shone.

"I'm hungry, mom," Monchi said, while playing with her brother Mati.

We returned to the house. On several occasions, we met workers who walked across the yard. Inside the house, we heard the conversations between my brothers and my mom. Some of my brothers and sisters had gone to work and others were returning home. The house had a bedroom for each of us even though each had our own big house.

Karincita was accustomed to bathing her children before dinner even though they had a nanny who looked after them. That evening I accompanied her. With the boy by one hand and the girl by the other, we walked down the corridor that led to the bathroom of their bedrooms.

We bathed them as they played with the water. The bathroom was large and old. The tub was next to a window overlooking the pool and garden. From the ceiling there hung a crystal chandelier. The walls were white with images of children. The pink marble floor was shining. The bathroom counter top was covered with a pink marble that covered the entire length of the bathroom wall. After we bathed the children, we dressed them and then had dinner. Then, we took them to bed. The beds of the children were facing a large window overlooking the garden and pool. The right side of the bedrooms of the children had shelves with toys for cognitive development.

The adults were talking in the dining room while the children had gone to sleep. Then, we had dinner with the rest of the family. That night after dinner, we went to the living room and a maid served us a delicious cognac.

"Victoria, we're happy you are with us," said Hugo, my older brother.

"Me too," I smiled.

I got along very well with Hugo because he was loving, but a little jealous of his younger sisters.

A while later, some of us went to bed while others continued talking. That night, I went to the library and continued writing. Then, Yannette went there sat on a sofa and continued reading a book.

CHAPTER IX

The next day, after breakfast, I went to my bedroom and opened the closet in which even after many years, there was still the clothing I wore as a teenager. The closet smelled musty. I looked at my low-cut floral dresses. I took out one, which was my favorite. That was the dress, which was the witness to my first seduction. Then, I threw a pile of dresses on the bed. I took a pink dress and tried it on. It still fit me. I smiled as I walked to and fro. I felt like a teenager again. It was a low-cut summer outfit. It reached down to the calves. On the shoulders, the dress had a strap on each side. I felt as when I was a teenager even though I was twenty-nine.

While remembering my teens, I heard the voices of the children of my niece Karincita. The children were playing and walking down the hallway. As they approached their bedrooms, I heard their voices again.

"Aunt Victoria, the dress looks beautiful on you!" my niece said when she appeared at the door.

I smiled and said, "Thank you; it's a dress I had when I was younger."

"Aunt, you look really good."

She always liked to make people feel good. Her children were beautiful, just like her. She had studied law for two years, but after she got pregnant when she married, she postponed her studies. Then she was going to continue studying. She had a great personality and could use it as a lawyer. Also, she liked to travel abroad, especially to Australia.

While talking with Karincita, her children climbed on the bed. When she heard them jumping on a pile of clothing, she said to them,

"No darlings, get down from the bed!"

"Let them play," I said smiling.

The children laughed as they jumped, but Karincita told them to stop jumping.

Through the window, I heard someone ask, "Where are the children?"

My niece walked up to the window, opened it, and saw the nanny.

"Brenda, don't worry . . . the children are with us."

"All right, ma'am."

A while later, the children took off their shoes and ran down the corridor to a stairway leading to the second floor. When they started running up the stairs, we walked into the living room and found my mom and Yannette on the terrace. We agreed to go walking in the garden.

"Children, let's go for a walk in the garden," Karincita said.

The children ran to the living room, playing and shouting happily where we were.

Under the high ceiling and marble hallway, we walked

with the children towards the garden. But then the children ran and jumped in front of us.

"Hi, Auntie Victoria, how are you?" Monchi said to me in English.

"Fine, thank you, and you?" I said hugging her.

"Very well."

The two children loved to talk to me in English.

Outside, we walked along a stone pathway into the garden. There, the birds were chirping.

"My father loved to walk in the backyard and garden," Yannette said.

From the garden, as we turned around, we looked at the family home that looked like a building. We remembered Christmas time.

"For Christmas, my father liked to decorate the Christmas tree," I said.

"Yes! The smell of Christmas was felt throughout the house," Yannette said.

"From the garden, through the open windows, we used to look at the big Christmas tree in the living room," my mother remembered.

The children ran around us while we talked. Yannette's daughters were talking with us. The birds chirped in the trees nearby. For a while, we talked about how we used to spend Christmas.

"For the workers and us, it was a very happy time to decorate the Christmas tree with my dad," my brother, Roberto, said.

"They knew that the *patron* placed gifts for every one of them at the foot of the Christmas tree," my mother said.

In that way, we remembered our father who was very traditional and affectionate.

"*Le fils de la Vierge, L'agneau Blanc* must have our father in the *Le Park du Champ Joli*," I said.

"Yes, in the heavenly and eternal paradise that the Virgin Mary has for all believers and followers of her Son Jesus Christ, *L'agneau Blanc*," Yannette said.

"It's Christian mythology that has inspired many writers," my mother said, who was an English teacher.

"I love that French poem," I said.

"Who wrote it?" Yannette asked.

"Jean de Meun wrote the second part of the poem *Le Roman de la Rose*, The Romance of the Rose," I said.

"Oh, yes, now I remember it," Yannette said.

"I like that poem because it is filled with images of nature and the extravagance of the European Middle Ages," my mother said.

"Me, too. I really like the courteous tradition that the poem shows," I said.

"The descriptions of the gardens with their fountains in the middle are very elegant," Yannette said.

Then we laughed when we heard some children happily talking to Max as if he had been a child. Max ran and jumped around the fence, barking softly to the children. There was a cold autumn breeze but we wore pants, sweaters, jackets and boots that day. Max was the tallest German shepherd in the town. Sometimes people spoke to him as if he were a child and asked him to give them avocados or almonds. Max barked softly and ran to get the things and gave it to them through the iron fence with his mouth. The children jumped up and down with pure joy as Max gave them fruits.

Then we continued talking about the medieval images.

"Returning to the conversation of the medieval gardens, the miraculous fountain in the garden of the Virgin Mary with the white lamb at the entrance is very interesting because they say that whoever looks at himself in the blessed water of the fountain is blessed with good health forever," I said.

"Yes, and it is similar to the water of the hot spring of the Virgin of Lavoree in France," Yannette said.

After a while in the garden, we returned home for lunch. On the way there, we spoke as we looked across the mansion.

"The house is very well kept," I said.

"Yes, it was renovated," Karincita said.

The maids looked at us and smiled as they cleaned the windows of the first and second floors.

As we approached the house, the door opened and one of my older sisters came out.

"How was the walk?"

"Great!" I said.

As we walked in the hallway with the children to their bedrooms, one after the other asked us if they could swim in the pool.

"No darlings," Karincita said.

"But mom!" Monchi cried.

"In the summer, you can swim here but not now because the water is too cold," Karincita replied.

"Yes, mom," Monchi and Mati said.

Once in the house, we went to their bedrooms to get some clothing to change them. Meanwhile, we heard voices. Yannnette's daughters walked down the hallway to the dining room talking. After we changed clothes for the children, we went to the dining room for lunch. We sat around the table.

"Victoria, how are you doing?" my mom asked.

"I feel very happy to be here, mom," I replied.

"The children are-fascinated with their aunt from the U.S." Karincita said.

I kissed each one and they told me,

"We love you Aunt Victoria."

"Speak to your aunt in English," Karincita told them.

"I love you, auntie," Monchi said laughing with joy.

"Thank you very much," I said.

That evening we had dinner together. The children showed me their English books and they read some pages. They began to learn English since babbling their first words. They had no accent. Also, in the school where they studied, they spoke English frequently. Sometimes from the United States, I sent them some English books that I wrote for them.

That night, before the children went to bed, we agreed to go skiing at Portillo on Friday that weekend. The children anxiously waited that day.

"You have to dress up warmly," one of my sisters said.

"I have to buy ski clothing," I said smiling.

My sister had a build similar to me and said she would lend me her ski clothing.

"Okay, thank you very much," I answered.

But we still went to Parque Arauco to buy ski clothing before going skiing

CHAPTER X

That weekend, we went to Portillo. It was Friday. We got up early, put the things in the Range Rover, and left. The sky was blue and the sun was shining everywhere. That day there was a lot of traffic and bustle in the city. An hour later, we took the freeway. Talking, we did not notice the passing time. Hours later, we drove up a curving hill to the ski resort. On the roadside, there were dried leaves.

We shuddered looking down from the height of the cliff. The tires were slipping on the slope. Through the windows, we could see the snow on the tops of the hills around us.

Then, we arrived at Portillo. We parked the vehicle and got out. The hotel employees came to greet us. They took the bags from the trunk and walked next to us to the resort. We had reservations for that weekend. After we checked in, we went to our rooms. The employees left the bags next to the closet and told us where things were in the rooms. Once they left, we looked around and put our clothes in the closet. The rooms were comfortable. The queen beds were big and had light blue bedspreads. On one of the white walls there hung a painting of skiers at Portillo. In front of the door, there were big windows covering almost the entire wall. From the ceiling of the rooms, there were lamps hanging. For a while, we stood in front of the window and looked out. Outside, we saw the beautiful lake, Laguna del Inca, completely frozen and skiers who walked beside it with their skis. Beyond that, we saw hills covered with snow.

After breakfast, we changed to ski clothes and headed for the lifts. That day, Portillo was lonely. The ski season had started recently. We skied for a while and when we were exhausted we returned to the hotel to rest.

That day we ate a delicious lunch. While we ate, I noticed a handsome man, with light skin, blue eyes, tall, and attractive, looking at me. My sister had told me his name was Pierre Lovell, but I told my sister, Yannette, that someone was looking at her from another table.

"Someone is looking at you," I said discretely.

"Since I'm a lawyer, many people know me," she replied.

With discretion, I looked at the person who was looking at our table. At that moment, our eyes met and we smiled at each other. A while later, Pierre stood on the pretext to greet my sister but it was to meet me.

"Hello Yannette," he said.

"What a surprise! I had no idea you were here! This is my sister Victoria who came from the United States," Yannette said.

"Pleased to meet you," I answered and he gave me a kiss on the cheek. Then, he greeted my sisters, brothers, nieces, and my mom.

"What a surprise, Pierre!" Yannette said again.

"I just came to relax."

"Are you alone?" my sister asked.

"Yes, I came alone!" Pierre replied with a loving smile.

"Why don't you join us?" Yannette said.

"I'd like to, but I have my lunch over there," he answered.

"Let's ski together in the afternoon," one of my brothers said.

"Sure," Pierre said.

When a waitress walked by Pierre, he told her to bring his plate to our table.

As we ate, Pierre looked at me repeatedly with his blue and seductive eyes. I thought he was of English descent for his elegance.

"How do you find the ski resort?" Pierre asked me.

"I love it," I said.

"Here, we can see the clear sky," one of my brothers said.

"It's unbelievable, the level of smog in Santiago," said Magaly, who loved to go skiing and go to hot springs.

We also heard other skiers who were talking in the restaurant.

"For how long are you going to stay in Chile?" Pierre asked me after I told him I came from Honolulu.

"For two months," I said.

"You'll enjoy Chile," he replied with a seductive smile.

"Yes, but I returned to Chile for my father," I answered a little depressed. "He just died."

We continued talking. In the afternoon, we went skiing. While we were skiing Pierre said,

"Did you have a hard time learning to ski?"

"No," I replied.

I told Pierre not to speak formally, but to call me Victoria.

"Yes, Victoria," Pierre said kindly.

For a while we talked about learning to ski. Pierre said he had learned to ski as a child so he was fascinated by the sport.

"Me too, since a little girl, I've been fascinated by that sport," I said smiling.

"Then, when I studied psychology for a semester at the Catholic University, I became more interested in the effects of sport," Pierre said.

"What did you study next?" I asked.

"Journalism, and you?" Pierre replied.

"I studied psychology, English, and French literature."

"How interesting!" Pierre said.

All of a sudden, I screamed when I slipped and almost fell, but Pierre quickly grabbed my arm to keep me from falling and in so doing he almost kissed me.

"Thank you, Pierre," I said, laughing.

"As a gentleman, I'm here to protect you," Pierre said.

I noticed that he liked me. I could not believe that I felt the same for him and found him very attractive.

"I hadn't skied for years," I said smiling as we continued skiing enthusiastically from one side to another. At the top of the hill, we were with other skiers. That day, the ski area was not very crowded. From the summit, we saw some people who were learning to ski. I thought that Pierre was friendly and lovely.

"You could teach those students how to learn to ski faster," Pierre said.

"Yes," I replied fascinated.

"Where did you study psychology?" he asked.

"At Cambridge University," I said.

"Cambridge?"

"Yes," I said.

"It's one of the most prestigious universities in the world," Pierre said.

"Yes! So that's why I decided to study there."

The snow was slippery. We laughed when we were skiing. The blue sky was clear. I looked around the valleys. We felt dizzy and had the fear of slipping. Sometimes, I thought about the novel "My Father" that I started writing during the flight to Chile. I felt warm skiing even though it was cold.

"Do you like skiing?" Pierre asked me.

"Yes, very much," I said smiling.

I was a little depressed, but I felt better when skiing beside Pierre and we looked and smiled at each other. I knew that dopamine was causing me a euphoric state of happiness or a feeling like falling in love because of the exercise.

Then, when I almost fell again, Pierre held me firmly by my arm for support. We looked into each other's eyes and laughed like children at play. Then, we continued skiing. Pierre thought I was the love of his life. When he saw that a skier looked at me constantly, Pierre looked at him jealously even though we were just beginning to know each other. Sometimes, he looked at my rosy cheeks and lips, but I made it seem as if I did not notice it. When we had skied for a few hours, we got hungry.

"Shall we go back for dinner?" one of my sisters said.

We ran to the ski lift. From the summit of the hill, we looked at other skiers in the snow-covered hills. The white mountain reminded me of Wordsworth's poem Le Mont Blanc or The White Mountain. The poem describes sensory experiences and pure ideas of the mind.

When we reached the ski lift, we went in groups. We heard laughter, screaming, and conversations.

"You look very pretty in the ski outfit," Pierre told me when we got on the ski lift and looked at my blue eyes.

I smiled.

Then, in groups we walked to the hotel. In our bedrooms, we sat on the beds taking off our ski clothes. The hotel was warm. Then, we returned to the hotel restaurant and had dinner together.

During dinner, Pierre looked at me seductively. I told him I was writing a novel.

"How interesting!" Pierre said.

"I hope you like it," I said.

'It's not the first she writes," one of my sisters said.

"What else have you written?" he asked me.

"Several, among them I wrote, *My Love Beyond The Labyrinth*," I said.

"In English?" Pierre asked.

"Yes," I said.

"Wow!"

We heard classical music while we ate and talked. We were at a table next to a window that had a beautiful view of the Laguna del Inca. There were large windows and a chandelier. That day, there were not many people.

"When I look at the snow, I think of an English poem that mentions the icebergs breaking off and falling with a loud sound like thunder," I said.

"Ah, it must be Coleridge's Ancient Mariner," Pierre said smiling.

"How do you know?" I asked curiously.

"I studied in England as a child," Pierre said.

"That's why you speak English with a British accent," I

said.

"Yes," Pierre said.

That night we talked until late. The next morning, I awoke before sunrise. When I looked through the window, I saw lots of snow and fog. For a while, I watched the snow thinking: "This is my first novel in Spanish." As I lie awake thinking about my novel, a stream of images and ideas came to my mind. Then, thinking about Pierre, I fell asleep again and dreamt that I was arriving in a Rolls Royce at a library of a university that I had built. At the library, I was signing autographs at a table covered with copies of my novel. Many people in groups were waiting for me. Some people wore caps with the name of my novel. Others shouted and clapped when my editor and I arrived at the library. We parked in front of the library at the university. A bodyguard opened the way for me among the many people to get there. The journalists approached the microphones to ask me questions.

"What do you think about the success of your novel?" one of them asked me.

"I'm very happy!" I answered.

Making my way, I answered the questions to the journalists. Inside the library, I stood before a table that was covered with my books. While signing autographs, some young people gave me a kiss on the cheek. When I had signed many autographs, I saw some youths reading scenes from my novel that they liked. One read a scene that said I had an English daughter. As I listened, I thought she was reading a scene from another novel I had written, but I said nothing. In my dream, after the presentation of my novel and book signing, the public applauded me and many people approached me to ask me questions about the novel. I continued dreaming that as I walked back to the car, a lot of people jostled to tell me something or ask me for autographs, journalists with their cameras focused on me and asked me questions.

CHAPTER XI

The next day at Portillo, when I awoke in the morning, there was thick fog and I could hardly see the hills covered with snow. As I wished it would not rain to go skiing with Pierre, it cleared and the sky looked deep blue. Then, the sun was shining in my room. For some time, I just laid in bed looking at the hills covered with snow as I thought about Pierre. Then, I smiled when I remembered the dream. I felt like a premonition that my novel would be a success. Pierre had gotten up already and was waiting for me in the dining room of the hotel talking with some of my brothers. Pierre smiled when he remembered the seduction of the previous day and could not wait to see me.

That morning I had breakfast with my family and Pierre. During breakfast, we showed one another the pictures we took the previous day. We giggled as we looked at them.

Later, we all went skiing. The sun was shining, but it was very cold. As we skied, Pierre whispered in my ear, "You look very beautiful."

Pierre and I spoke with excitement as we skied.

Before dusk, we returned to the restaurant and dined. As Pierre smiled looking at me lovingly as we ate, I started to feel less sad and depressed by the death of my father. During dinner, Pierre and I exchanged our phone numbers.

Then, we returned to Santiago. There was a lot of traffic. Many people blew their horns in the traffic jam. Back home, I wondered if Pierre would call me. While in his house, he thought that I fascinated him more than he realized and could not wait to see me and ask me to go out with him. In the house, we sat on a white sofa in the living room to watch videos and photographs of the family. First, Magaly, my older sister showed me the video of the wedding of her daughter, Karincita. My niece and her husband had celebrated their wedding at the casino for the Air Force officers. They looked very elegant. She was dressed in a white gown and he, as a lieutenant was in the uniform of an Air Force officer for the occasion. Several officers were dressed in full uniform and paid homage with their sabers up. All family and friends were in dressy clothes and all looked very happy.

"Karincita and her husband look very elegant," I said happily.

"You could have come to her wedding," Magaly said.

"Yes," I said.

After I saw the videos of the wedding, I saw another video on the wheat harvesting in the country of Yungay, when my father was well. He seemed very happy next to his workers, while the dogs ran through the wheat straw, and partridges that were there, came out of their nests and rose to fly a short distance away.

In the scene of the video, the day was very nice. The sky was blue, and the wheat was yellow while the machine harvested the wheat.

"He gave work to many people who needed to take advantage of the season," my mother said.

"What will happen to those workers?" I said.

Later, the front door of the house opened and my brother Hugo who was tall, blond and with brown eyes came in.

"Hello, what are you doing?" he asked graciously.

"We're looking at pictures," one of my sisters said.

While looking at the pictures, Pierre called me on my cellular but I did not answer it because I had left it in my room. So he called my home. When the phone rang, one of my brothers stood to answer it. It was Pierre, but he did not ask for me but pretended to be a stranger and having the wrong number because he was afraid that I could reject him. I was happy to be with my family again. Then, we became hungry and we had dinner.

"We could go to the country in the south," my mother said.

"Yes mom . . . I'd love it!" I exclaimed.

In the summer, my family used to go to the house in Yungay. It was a custom among the rich people who had land in the south of Chile. Many relatives used to visit us there in the summer. The family's children loved to play in the hay at that time.

In that way we spent the night when we returned from Portillo.

The next morning, I got up very early to continue writing my novel. For a while, I sat behind my desk in the library and when I had written two chapters, I went down to have breakfast with my family. When I returned to my desk, Pierre called me.

"Hi, I'm Pierre," he said.

"How are you?" I said.

"I called to invite you to have lunch with me," Pierre said.

I said I was busy writing my novel, but would accept his invitation.

"Would it be okay if I pick you up at twelve?" Pierre asked me.

"All right."

When he arrived at the house, I was not ready yet, so he sat on a sofa in the living room and waited for me. He invited me to have lunch at a fancy restaurant in Vitacura. On the way there, we talked about many things.

"You look worried," Pierre said.

"Yes, a bit . . . because of the novel."

Actually, I was depressed by the death of my father and still had not overcome that.

In the restaurant, we sat at a table next to a window. Suddenly, it began to drizzle and I looked out. The restaurant was not crowded. The food was delicious. We had filet mignon with rice and red wine. His blue eyes seemed bluer in the light of the sun through the drizzle.

"How is your novel coming along?" Pierre asked me.

"Good," I replied.

"You'll do very well," Pierre said.

I smiled and said, "I hope so . . . God willing."

Then we talked about other things.

"Why did you study journalism?" I asked.

"I love to inform the public about events that interest them."

"Was it difficult to learn how to write news?" I asked.

"No, because I easily learned the structure of how to write them, for example, first you start with the title of the news and then the first paragraph that answers the basic questions: who, what, when, where, and why, etc." he replied.

That made me remember when I studied journalism in the United States and said,

"I remember that I found the logic to write the news interesting."

Pierre was surprised and smiled as he realized how much we had in common. I thought the only difference was that I had learned it in English while he learned it in Spanish.

"In English we call the five basic questions, the five wh-questions," I said.

And in that way while we ate and talked, Pierre looked at me in a loving way and little by little I felt less depressed.

Soon after, we were silent but happy with each other.

"What are you thinking?" Pierre asked me.

"If you only knew," I said smiling.

Pierre smiled because he was very happy with me. He said I was much nicer than he thought.

A while later, we left the restaurant and as we walked to his vehicle, he invited me to his house. Outside, it was raining heavily. Pierre opened his umbrella and I snuggled up next to him and ran through the rain in the parking lot to the car. Sometimes he spoke to me, but I could not hear him because of the rain.

At his home, we were soaking wet, so Pierre gave me a large sweater to wear. While he went to change his clothes in his bedroom, I was putting on his sweater. I giggled when I realized it was baggy.

"Wow it looks like a miniskirt," Pierre said with a warm smile.

We both laughed a little bit.

Then we sat in the living room. Pierre offered me something to eat but I was not hungry because we had just eaten. Then I accepted a warm glass of milk. The sound of the rain could be heard from the terrace.

Pierre felt passionate to have me in his house and looked at me vulnerable with his sweater.

When my sweater and pants were dry, I put them on in the bathroom, and I told him to take me home.

"I have to go home," I said.

"It's raining," Pierre said.

"It will rain all day," I said.

"Why don't you stay?" Pierre asked.

I looked at him and said, "I have to go."

His eyes shone with excitement. I knew what would happen if I stayed. Therefore, I pretended that I did not feel the same. He already saw himself unbuttoning my white cashmere sweater and my blouse under it.

We left. He took me to my house. Upon arrival, quickly I sat at the table while Pierre returned home. My family was waiting for me to have dinner. Pierre, upon reaching his home, sat on a sofa in his living room and drank a glass of whiskey as he imagined kissing me. During dinner, I pretended that I had not wanted to stay with Pierre, while Pierre's only thoughts were of being with me.

During that week, we met several times. One day, we met in the garden of the house of my family. As we walked talking, Pierre spoke to me lovingly. Suddenly when no one was around, he tried to hold my hand, but I pulled it away pretending that I did not want it. But then I let him take my hand and he asked me to be his girlfriend. I accepted it because I felt happy with him. He kissed me and told me that he had fallen in love with me at first sight. Pierre liked me very much. That afternoon, we kept our romance a secret. I did not want to tell my family yet. But days later, Pierre and I told my family about it.

The first week went by very fast. I compared my life there; which was like being in the richness of the Middle Ages and my life in the United States, where I lived in a penthouse apartment in Waikiki in front of the beach. In both places, there were many trees that swayed in the breeze and I felt attachment for both places.

Another day in the afternoon, as my family, some relatives, and friends sat on sofas in the living room, we talked of many things. They never got tired inviting me to their homes and various places. They wanted me to acculturate to our country.

"Sister, Victoria, what happened with Pierre," Hugo said.

"He's okay," I said smiling.

Then Roberto, whom we called "Titin," and had studied computer science came in and told me he had already overcome his depression. He administered the estate of my father and wanted to return to college. He told me many interesting things. Some of my aunts told me about their farms, their children, and grandchildren. Many of my nephews had gone into a career in law. Some had studied psychology. Others were teachers and taught in universities or colleges.

Among the nieces was Montserrat, who loved to comb her hair and was very choosy about clothing and Matthew who spoke like a physician because his grandfather had taught him many things about medicine.

CHAPTER XII

The days passed in that way. After a week or so, when I had written several chapters of the novel, I called several publishers. Many answered me, but I chose the most prestigious one.

Another day while having lunch with my family, I heard the phone ringing in the living room. One of the workers answered it and said "Miss, Victoria, an editor is calling you."

I hurried to answer the phone. After greeting the editor, he said he was interested in my novel.

"I'd like to read the manuscript of your novel," he said.

For me, it was like a dream that one of the most prestigious publishers was calling me. We agreed to get together on Thursday in two weeks at ten o'clock at a restaurant. The editor of this publisher liked to meet writers at fancy restaurants.

When I hung up the phone, I still could not believe it. In the afternoon, for a while I sat on a sofa in the living room to correct any errors that could have been in the manuscript.

That afternoon, the fireplace heated the house. My mom was watching TV and some of my brothers were reading in their rooms. My sister Yannette was a lawyer and sometimes she was late when some clients invited her to celebrate in restaurants when she won their cases.

That evening, some of my brothers, my mom, and I had dinner together. During dinner, Yannette arrived. She greeted us saying,

"Hello! How are you?"

I smiled and said, "A publisher called me."

"Great!"

With the novel in hand, I asked her to read it to tell me how it was. She told me she was going to read it right away.

As we ate, Pierre called me on my cellular.

"I'm Pierre," he said with a loving voice.

"Hi Pierre, how are you?" I answered as I stood and excused myself as I walked to the living room.

"I have an invitation to go to the Municipal Theater to listen to Beethoven and I'd like you to come with me," Pierre said.

"When?" I asked.

"This weekend," Pierre said excitedly.

"Thank you for your invitation, but I cannot. I have to correct my novel because it was accepted by one of the best publishers," I said.

"Come, join me!" Pierre said.

"I love classical music, but I cannot," I said.

"Tell me another reason," Pierre said.

"I have to correct the manuscript of my novel," I insisted.

"I can help you correct it," Pierre said.

"Well, all right," I said.

He told me he was going to pick me up that weekend.

As I walked back into the dining room, I thought it would be great for me to go to the theater and listen to classical music and relax. I still felt depressed and had not overcome the death of my father

CHAPTER XIII

The day of the invitation, as I put on my makeup, I smiled and giggled thinking how well I would enjoy being with Pierre. When he picked me up to go to the Municipal Theater, I smiled and he said with a kiss, "You look very beautiful in that beige gown and hat." That evening, Pierre looked very attractive in a dark suit, white shirt, and maroon tie. During the drive, we felt good and excited talking about one another. At the theater, as we walked in, we greeted other people dressed in gowns. In the hall of the Municipal Theater, many people were talking or having a cocktail. One of them approached us and said, "There will be a very good performance." "I hope so," Pierre said. For a while, we talked and then I was left alone with Pierre. We sat in a row in front of the orchestra. The side seats were vacant, but then they were filled.

"Do you like classical music?" Pierre asked me.

"Yes, I love it," I said.

"Do you often go to listen to the symphony in Hawaii?" he asked.

"In the past, I often went, but now I'm too busy with my work."

"How often do you write?" he asked.

"I write in my notebook anywhere when I have time," I answered.

Minutes later we began to hear the music. All the musicians were behind their instruments. We immediately stopped talking to focus on the music. The symphony began with "Beethoven's Symphony No. 9 in G minor," which was very soothing.

When tears ran down my cheeks as I listened to the music, Pierre took my hand and told me to enjoy the music. I smiled and continued listening. The music triggered fond memories of my family listening to classical music on the pool deck, surrounded by flowers. My father enjoyed walking or sitting, reading a book as he listened to classical music and occasionally looked across at the garden with rosebushes and beyond at the fruit trees.

During the intermission, we talked for a while. Then, we walked to the lobby at the entrance to have a cocktail.

"How did you find the performance?" Pierre asked me.

"Magnificent."

We drank a strawberry cocktail while we stood and talked. Then, we returned to the next presentation of the orchestra. While waiting for the musicians to begin, we talked.

"How is your novel going?" Pierre asked me again, knowing that it was very important to me.

"I have to edit some things," I said.

"You'll be a famous writer when you publish it," Pierre said.

I smiled and said, "Hopefully, God willing."

The presentation of the symphony orchestra lasted two hours. Then, we left the theater and walked towards the parking lot. On the way home, Pierre drove and I sat beside him. Along the way, we talked with excitement

"I like you," he said.

I pretended that I did not hear and looked outside.

"Why are you not saying anything? Don't you like me?" he asked.

"Don't say that," I said.

"Why not?" He asked distressed.

"Because you know that you like me."

Later it started to drizzle. The drops of water looked like crystals on the glass. Soon, Pierre turned on the windshield wipers as the radio started playing an English romantic song.

"Do you like the song?" Pierre asked me.

"Yes, I love it," I replied. "Would you mind if I turn up the volume?"

"Of course not," he answered.

As we heard the song, he tried to kiss me, but I backed away. I thought I was not sure of my romance with him.

"What's the matter?" he said.

"Nothing," I replied.

"Why do you reject me?" Pierre said.

"No, I don't reject you."

Sometime later, Pierre tried to kiss me again. This time, he took my hand first and then kissed me. I could not believe it. He liked me, but I was afraid to fall in love with him because I knew I had to return to the United States. He begged me to go to his house, but I told him to take me home.

I returned home not too late. My brothers and my mom

were sitting at the dining table. I joined them. That night, there was chicken soup with peas and peach cobbler.

"How was the presentation?" Yannette asked.

"Spectacular," I replied.

"Victoria has always loved classical music," my mother said.

"Yes, it's true, Mom," I said.

After an hour or so, we stood up from the table. I went upstairs to the library and sat behind my desk to revise what I had written in the morning. I took the manuscript of my novel that was in front of me. While reading, I took a pen and started to correct any errors.

Then for a while, I stood in front of the big window and looked out. I heard the sounds of crickets while some leaves blew on the tennis court. I liked hearing the sound of the foliage of the trees.

Then my sister, Yannette, went to the library for a law book. We talked as she skimmed through the book and I looked outside.

"How is Pierre?" Yannette asked.

"He's nice," I said.

"Don't you find his blue eyes too big?" She said smiling.

"I love them."

Then I showed her a picture of Pierre and me on my cellular.

"He has a big mouth," Yannette said.

I smiled and said, "But he kisses very tenderly!"

"Well, it's your taste," Yannette said smiling.

"Poor thing!" I sighed thinking about how it must have burned his ears.

"I noticed that he really likes you," Yannette said.

"Perhaps," I smiled pretending that I had not realized that.

"Why not?" My sister replied.

That night, while Pierre leaned back in his bed thinking about me, he tried to call me. But, he was afraid of being too pushy. He took the phone, but quickly hung up. He tried to sleep but could not. He could not fall asleep as his mind jumped from one thought to another thinking about me.

The next morning, over breakfast in the dining room on the first floor, my family and I agreed to go to the country estate of Yungay on Friday that weekend.

CHAPTER XIV

The night before going to the south, Pierre had dinner with us. He wanted to go there with us, but said he had to read the news very early the next day. As we ate and talked enthusiastically in the main dining room, some workers packed the bags. They put in our winter clothing, pajamas, toothbrushes, etc. After some time, a maid went to tell us that she had packed everything.

"Children go to bed so you don't oversleep tomorrow morning! Pierre can stay in one of the guest rooms," my mother said, standing at the table.

"Yes, mom," we replied.

"Mom, let's talk a bit more," Yannette said.

"Children, go to bed!" my mother said again.

"But mom!" Yannette said.

Carmen, one of the older sisters said, "Yes kids, let's go to bed." Hearing her, one after another we stood and some of us went to bed.

Pierre and I went to the balcony and looked out. I shivered in Pierre's arms as we spoke and kissed. It was cold on the balcony and the wind shook the branches of the trees and at times it howled. Then, as we looked out, I heard my mom say, "Children go to bed."

"I must go to bed," I said as he did not let me go.

"Not yet," Pierre said.

"I have to get up early tomorrow," I said.

"You know that I love you," he said.

"Why don't you come with us?" I asked.

"My love, I have to read the news very early tomorrow," he said.

"Okay."

"Aren't you going to see me off?" he said.

He kissed me time after time and said, "When you think of me, look at the cellular because it is going to be my energy of love that reaches you."

I smiled and said, "Your energy of love, so do you have telepathic powers?"

"My energy of love can reach you telepathically anywhere, my love!" he said.

We laughed a little and then he kissed me passionately and he left and I went to my bedroom thinking about Pierre and the journey to the south the next day.

Minutes later as was taking off my sweater, sitting on my bed, Pierre called me to tell me he loved me. Then, I got into bed.

CHAPTER XV

The next morning, everyone was up at sunrise. It was the first time in many years that I was going to the country estate in the South. As I brushed my hair in my bedroom, one of my sisters peered through the door and said, "Hi, Victoria, they are going to serve breakfast."

Soon, I went downstairs to have breakfast with the rest of my family. My family was there sitting around the table, except my father. After breakfast, we left excitedly towards Yungay. The morning was nice although the sun had not risen yet. The Range Rover that was my father's favorite vehicle ran smoothly. It was Friday and the streets were deserted. We passed big houses on either side of the street. Then, we entered some narrow streets. People dressed in parkas and coats were waiting for buses on both sides of the street. About an hour later, we entered the freeway filled with vehicles. Some cars passed at high speed while sunshine entered the windows. During the journey, we talked to pass the eight hours it took to reach the country estate.

"What's that ringing?" I asked as we drove down the freeway.

"Those rings mark the tacs which determines the price that you pay for using the freeway," Yannette replied.

"What?" I asked curiously.

"A Spanish company manages the freeway," Hugo said.

"I can't believe that," I said a little upset.

"Now you pay to go on the freeway and park in the shopping malls," said my sister Magaly, who was very nationalistic and defended Chilean things a lot.

"I think in the United States, the freeways and parking lots would never be managed by foreigners," I said upset.

We could hear the roar of the engines of buses and trucks coming from the windows.

"What can we do?" Hugo said.

"In any case, it's better than to ride the bus," I said disappointed.

"With the *tacs* and expensive gasoline, I don't even have money to buy food," Carmen said irritated.

"I think it was a very bad decision to have given control and power of the freeways to foreigners," I said angrily.

"What can we do now?" one of my brothers said.

"Did the Chilean people participate in the decision to transfer power of the freeway to foreigners?" I asked.

One of my brothers said, "Sister, now, only a few make decisions in Chile."

"Anyway, the Panamericana Freeway is still ours," I said.

The sound of the *tacs* made me furious. When I left for the United States there were not those nasty *tacs* that felt like scratching one's head. I was desperate for what was happening in my country. I felt like telling my family to emigrate to the United States or England. Not only I was furious that many people had no money to pay for *tacs*, but also to see that in Chile there was a huge difference between the high and low social classes. The middle class suffered the most. I wondered if rich company owners did something to improve the condition of the poor and middle classes by giving to charities. While riding in the Range Rover, I thought about some reports of Chile I had seen in the United States. In one of them, I saw many poor immigrants that the United States rejected, but who were accepted in Chile with many benefits which not even the poor, born and raised in Chile had. I pretended not to feel angry about the injustice to many Chileans. The human condition in my country was very bad with violence, poverty, and poor education. I thought of preventions and interventions to improve the human condition, especially for children and the elderly, who were the most vulnerable, which I could do with help from the United States.

In the news, they often showed reports about people unhappy with the Chilean investment in used buses that were supposed to be new. The government did not stop people from expressing their discontent with the buses that often broke down and the neglect to improve living conditions because many children lived in unsanitary, dirty, and cold tents in ghettos. Food was almost the same price as in the United States and of not very good quality. This infuriated me and I wondered why nobody did anything to improve the harsh conditions.

I did not want to get involved in politics, but I was thinking from a utilitarian point of view after I saw so much poverty especially among children. I thought that it was a bad decision to allow so many poor immigrants from war-torn countries who were on welfare. I had been in the United States too long to tolerate so many abuses. Many of the poor and middle classes had lost benefits. I was very rich, but I did not have so much money to help so many poor people.

Then we passed a few restaurants, on both sides of the road. From them came the smell of meat pies and cakes. When we got hungry, we stopped in front of one. We parked in front of the entrance door. Upon entering the restaurant, we smiled as we heard pleasant folk music. A waitress led us to a table near a window. Some of us asked for the same food, fresh cheese, cake, homemade bread, fresh milk, and meat pies with salad.

We talked while we waited for the food. Several people were leaving or entering the restaurant. Soon, the waitress appeared with trays. The table had a tablecloth with floral designs. The waitress put a basket with rolls in the center of the table. I took one and put blackberry and peach marmalade on it.

"You like that!" Yannette said.

"For many years, I had not tasted something so good," I answered smiling.

"I'm hungry!" Hugo said, pulling out one of the homemade hot rolls.

The bread was fresh and the milk was hot. Some of my brothers took lumps of sugar from the sugar bowl and put it in the hot milk and then took bread and spread marmalade on it. The waitress put a lot of blackberry marmalade on the table. It was my favorite marmalade because during the summers I loved eating blackberries with my brothers and sisters in the brambles of the estate.

As the morning sun streamed through the window, Pierre called me and asked me if I had missed him. I said "Yes," and that in a certain way he was right that many times I tried to read his mind when I used my intuition to find out what he was doing. The spoons clinked on the cups as my family and other people mixed the milk with sugar.

"The breakfast is delicious!" one of my brothers said.

"Very good!" Hugo said.

Then my nieces wanted to buy gum, but my sister told them that the girls looked terrible chewing, especially when blowing big bubbles.

"But Mom, we're not going to make bubbles," Kati said graciously.

The others smiled thinking many times when we stuck gum on our clothing and we had a hard time taking it off.

Then, we changed the topic of conversation.

"What would you think if I had a mustache?" my brother Hugo asked.

"Are you kidding?" I said graciously.

"No," Hugo said.

"You must be kidding because you don't want to look macho," I said.

"Macho? Don't you find them sexy?" Hugo said smiling.

We laughed because none of us liked mustaches because we found them ugly.

Sometime later, when I looked out the window, I saw a beggar asking for money. Then I thought how it was possible for a country to accept so many immigrants instead of helping our Chilean disadvantaged. In the United States, many people criticized Chile because it accepted many foreign immigrants that the United States would never accept.

After breakfast, we stood and walked out towards the Range Rover. Then, we continued our journey to the country. The vehicle was going about 80 miles per hour on the highway Five South. It was very noisy, so we closed the windows. The radio played a song that was popular in Chile and in the United States. Hugo turned up the volume and Yannette turned it even higher.

"Not so loud," Hugo said.

"Your father loved this song," my mother said.

CHAPTER XVI

We arrived in Chillan around eleven o'clock in the morning. Upon arriving there, we saw some students who walked on both sides of the street with their books. Later, we went through downtown. The sun was shining. My brother Hugo filled the tank with gasoline. Then, we crossed the center of Chillán. After we left the city, we entered a narrow road towards Yungay. Sometimes, the Range Rover shook on the rough roads. While looking around, I thought of the country descriptions for my novel. That day was not very cold.

Later, we reached a narrow street with houses with cardboard on the windows. When the Range Rover turned right, we entered into heavy traffic. On both sides of the street, people walked with colorful clothes. Smoke came out from the chimneys of the houses.

The vehicle reduced speed when we spotted a cart drawn by oxen on the street, which was very common in the country. Further ahead, we saw some old houses. Then, we passed many fields. On either side of the road, there were trees with swaying branches with yellow leaves. Some men riding horses nodded their heads to say hello. The breeze was fresh. People went in and out of their homes. It was early when we approached the town. There was a lot of traffic. Vehicles were traveling in both directions. Sometimes, we could see men on horses wearing traditional country clothing riding alongside the road. Further ahead, we could see several farms with houses distinct from each other. Then, the Range Rover approached the bridge called Trilaleo and then another bridge called Panqueco. We smelled smoke coming from the chimneys of the houses along the road. The road rose and soon we reached the Plaza of Yungay. I was happy to be there after so many years. My brother stopped the Range Rover on one side of the plaza and we got out to stretch our legs. The plaza was unchanged. It was as I remembered it, with many tall linden trees with golden leaves. In the autumn, the lindens changed their leaves from green to yellow brown, on all four sides of the plaza. The only change I noticed was that on one side, there were two new restaurants now. From the outside they looked empty.

"How happy I am to be here, after so many years!" I said emotionally. The plaza was as beautiful as before.

"Victoria, your father often came to this church on Sundays," my mom said when we passed it alongside the plaza.

Many leaves had fallen and blew with the breeze on the concrete walkways. The flowers had some petals. Green grass, tinged with brown covered the gardens on the edges of the plaza. There were green wooden benches. On some of them were wet leaves fallen from the trees. That day, many people walked around the plaza while we looked around and talked. Yungay was very beautiful. Often, we could hear the conversations of others who were nearby. Some people greeted my mother, my brothers, and my sisters, but they did not recognize me and neither did I recognize them. When my mother told them I was her daughter Victoria visiting from the U. S., they embraced me. A while later, we left the plaza. On the way home, I looked at the swaying trees on both sides of the street in front of the big old houses. Ahead, when we were arriving at the big house, tears started running down my face. I did not want anyone noticing it, even though the feeling of being in my hometown was very, very deep.

CHAPTER XVII

The Range Rover stopped in front of the gate to where the house was about a block inside. The workers who were in the garden ran to open the gate.

"Good morning," one of them said.

"How are you?" we answered.

As we entered and went up the driveway with tall trees that led to the mansion, I was filled with sadness as I thought I would never see my father again. Then we saw the tall white pillars at the entrance and they were pretty much as before. Then suddenly, when we approached the house, the door opened and my younger brother Robert who was a bachelor, appeared. My brother, who had an elegant English appearance, smiled and walked quickly to meet us. We got out of the Range Rover and greeted each other with a hug and kiss. Robert had traveled to the south days before and had told the maids to cook our favorite foods.

Workers helped us with the bags as we walked towards

the entrance of the house. We walked down a wide hallway with high ceilings and marble floors to the living room. Other workers greeted us as we passed. The living room was just as I remembered it, with a huge crystal chandelier hanging from the ceiling. Inside some of us sat on sofas while others went to the bathroom. The sun entered through the large windows that opened to balconies on the second floor. The walls of the house were painted white and they were pictures and paintings of famous painters. The house was full, but we felt the absence of our father. Now, there was only his memory. Portraits of mom and dad hung on the wall to the right. It was when they were young. On a cabinet, I saw a picture of me when I was about five years old with my brothers, sisters, and parents. It was a picture when we visited our relatives in England. Sometimes, we could hear the chirping of the thrushes in the garden. The two-story mansion was almost as before.

"How do you find the house, Victoria?" my mom asked.

"Very nice, it's just as I remembered it," I answered.

"We could show the house to Victoria," Yannette said.

"I'd like to see it," I said. "There must be some changes and I would like to familiarize with it again."

Inside the house, one could hear our conversations and the workers who were happy to see me after so many years, but sad about my father.

In the main dining room, we sat at the table to have breakfast. Then, we ate breakfast. As we ate, we chatted missing our father. Some family portraits hung on the walls in the dining room, as if they were gazing over the dining table.

"The house is kept almost as before," I said as I looked at

my mother.

"Yes, Dad took great care of it," Yannette said.

After breakfast, we left the house to get some fresh air. Outside, it looked a little different. They had cut down the large apple tree, but there was a tall walnut tree fully grown in its place. It still had walnuts. As we walked through the yard, a dog barked.

"He's our dog, Max," mother said.

Seconds later, Max, appeared wagging his tail and playfully approached me and then jumped at me. I knew that it was a natural behavior for dogs when they felt happy to see someone.

"He doesn't bite!" my mom exclaimed, smiling.

Then when Max looked at me attentively, I stretched my hand to him to say, "Hi," and he lifted his right paw and I shook it saying, "Good Max." I giggled a little when Max licked my hand. My mother said, "Max is very happy to see you." Then, we walked by the side of the pool talking. Ahead, as we reached the garden, the garden gate opened and some workers came out.

"Good afternoon. Don't be afraid of the guardian," the workers said laughingly thinking that I was probably scared of Max. Max had grown and now looked almost like a bear.

Hugo joked, "Max barks, but doesn't bite."

"Yes sir!" a worker said.

My mother said petting her dog, "Max wants to play." My mother picked up a stick from the ground and threw it for Max to get it. Max ran after the stick and brought it back to my mother's feet. My mother said, "Excellent, Max." My mother loved to praise her dog for good behavior.

We spent an hour there. Then one of the workers told us

that lunch was ready. As we walked my mother told me that German shepherds had very helpful behavior and I agreed because I had studied it in animal behavior psychology.

At home, we sat around the dinner table on the first floor to have lunch. It had a white tablecloth and napkins of the same color and silverware. In the center of the table was placed bread baskets with bread, two bottles of red wine, juices, water, and salads . . . all in great abundance.

"How beautiful is Yungay," I said.

"Don't you find it changed?" my mom asked.

"Yes, a little," I replied.

"It's now more populated," Titin said.

"Yes, of course," Carmen said.

It seemed like a dream to be here after so many years. My brothers had not changed at all. As always the food was delicious.

Before we finished lunch, we agreed to go to the farm the next day. After lunch, we toured the house. We started on the first floor. We walked around the house for two hours. Later, we went for a ride by car.

"Your dad loved everything in the house," my mother said.

"That's why he was always repairing it," Robert said.

The dining room was just as I remembered it, with its chandelier hanging from the high ceiling. The clean white walls had been painted recently. On one wall was a portrait of the family with some of us mounted on white horses, while others posed on the side in front of the mansion. There was a photograph of my family, my brothers and sisters, and I, on a cabinet in a classic silver frame. We were children. My blond hair hung around my shoulders; one of my sisters had long golden curls. We were dressed in equestrian clothing. As I looked at the photograph, my mother told me that they had taken that photograph when my father bought ponies for us. The front wall had large windows. We entered the first floor bedrooms. They were pretty much as usual with large closets and white walls with pictures of us in the countryside and wildlife paintings.

In the bedroom of my father, we stopped. Then, I went to his nightstand, where the Bible that he loved so much to read was still there. His clothes were still in the closets and drawers. When I looked at his clothes, I imagined he was in the house. Tears welled up in my eyes. Then, I went to a shelf full of books that he had. There were many medical books, but like me he also liked to read English literature. When I took a Wordsworth's book, I realized that my dad was passionate about English romantic literature. A book by Hemingway seemed to have been read over and over again. When we were kids, my father loved to read to us. Sometimes in the summer, we sat on wheat straws to read books that my father bought for us. Next to the Bible, I saw the image of the Saint San Sebastian and the Virgin Mary with baby Jesus.

"So in that way our Lord Jesus Christ must be protecting our father in the paradise of God," I said.

"Our father was very compassionate," Yannette said.

Outside we could hear the workers talking. Some of them had swollen eyes from so much crying. My father was a very good employer to them, so now they mourned his absence.

"Victoria, your father stood in front of this window to look at the garden," my mother said.

"Yes, he loved the plants and trees very much and especially the rosebushes," I said.

Among the books he had on the shelf, I found the ones that I had written. I took them and smiled when I saw the notes next to the paragraphs that he liked. Then, I took more books on English and French classic literature, which were his favorites. As a good intellectual, he had volumes of psychology. My father loved to analyze his dreams from the point of view of Freud's psychoanalysis or Wundt's introspection. Among the books and articles on children's cognitive development, I found pages with logical reasoning exercises since the time he taught us the logic of mathematics learning. On a sheet of paper he had exercises with basic logic to understand the inverse property of addition. My father told us that children had to learn the logic of mathematics for a good foundation to learning.

Then, I left the room and walked around the house with the rest of my family. In the hallway, we stood to look and comment on the portraits from our childhood. Talking, we walked upstairs to the second floor. There were more bedrooms, bathrooms, a dining room, a living room and a library. The bedrooms and bathrooms were as before. The living room seemed bigger. The chandeliers hanging from the ceilings were the same. In the library, we stopped and looked at the books that filled it. In front of large windows that opened to balconies, there was a desk. When I was a girl, I used to climb on top of it and write in my diary because when I sat on the chair, the desk was too high. For a while, we skimmed through some books. As I looked at some literature, my brothers and my mom did the same. The house had the same meaning for everyone in the family. When we finished walking around the house, we went for a walk outside. We saw some workers raking up the leaves in the yard.

That evening at dinner, we agreed to go to the farm the next day. The farm was about an hour from Yungay. After dinner, we all stood up and went to bed.

CHAPTER XVIII

The next day we got up early before sunrise to go to the farm that was about a half hour from Yungay. Through the living room window, we heard the chirping birds settled in the trees and the sound of crickets hiding in the grass of the garden. That morning, we helped load all the bags and then got into the Range Rover. Next, we headed to the farm. We passed large houses that looked like ours. Ahead, we turned left and entered a wide road. As we approached the house, we saw countrywomen walking with their children along the roadside. The children's noses had mucus running down and some of them were barefoot.

The Range Rover rocked from side to side when we drove over the potholes in the roads that were covered with mud. Other vehicles squeaked as they passed over the bumpy road. It was early and we smelled garlic and fried onions coming from some houses. The farmers must have been having breakfast. On both sides of the road, the trees had lost their leaves and swayed in the breeze.

Later, we saw cows and horses grazing in the fields. Suddenly, among the trees and bushes on the right side of the road, a white rabbit appeared and ran in front of the vehicle. My brother slowed down fascinated, watching the rabbit, but the rabbit disappeared into the bushes. Soon, we spotted the entrance to the farm with its large gate. The sun was rising. The birds began to fly from the trees. Workers were walking down the path alongside the orchard. The long driveway with trees on the sides led to the two-story mansion. When a worker saw us, he hurried to meet us. He opened the iron gate and we entered. The name of the estate was Manchester. From the vehicle, we saw white and brown horses grazing.

"Good morning," one of the workers said.

"Good morning, how are you?" we answered smiling.

The driveway remained almost the same as years ago. The fruit orchard still had its fruit trees. On the ground were many wet, loose, and muddy leaves. On the right, we could see tall chestnut and oak trees. We parked the Range Rover in the yard and we got out. There was silence, since it was early morning. Some of the workers had risen while others slept. When some of them saw us through the windows, they ran out and greeted us tearfully. Then, as we walked to the entrance of the house, a worker opened the door. We entered and walked under a high ceiling hallway with marble floor to the living room. The living room looked like before, from the ceiling hung a crystal chandelier. Some workers took the bags to the bedrooms and we sat in the living room and talked for a while.

Then, we went to the dining room for breakfast.

Later, I went upstairs to the balcony of the living room

with some of my brothers. For a while, we looked outside at the backyard. Some birds were preening their feathers in the fountain in the garden, while the leaves of the trees floated in the pool and blew across the tennis court.

"Hi, what a beautiful day!" I said to a worker sweeping the leaves in the yard.

"Miss Victoria, what a surprise to see you!" the worker said rushing to hug me.

Then, we went downstairs and walked to the backyard. In the garden, we looked at the fountain were birds were chirping and preening their feathers while the dogs wagged their tails next to us. After we passed the garden next to the pool, we smelled manure coming from the stable. As we walked, we recalled that in the summer our Dad had a pony for us to ride. Then we went to see the orchard where the trees were covered with fruits in the summer. Now, the trees had few leaves. Sometimes, we could see the workers. They have worked there for a long time, so they were regarded as part of the household.

"The workers take very good care of the farm and are very loyal to us," my mother said and my brothers nodded in agreement.

"Yes, they became attached to us," I said.

With my mother and my brothers, we remembered the happy childhood we had in the house of the big farm. When we returned to the house for lunch, we saw a white truck parked next to the garden that my father used sometimes to go around the estate.

"Sister, do you remember when we used to climb in that cherry tree?" Robert said smiling.

"Yes, of course," I said.

We still could see some cherries.

After lunch, we went to the library. We started in the literature section and I stopped next to a shelf on the right to get a book. The others also took books and skimmed through them. Then, we went to sit on sofas beside the desk that was in front of the window. I opened a book of poems by Claire that had beautiful descriptions of the country. I read aloud a poem on nature. The poem described nature, as it was, natural and real.

"He wrote very well," one of my brothers, said.

A while later, I stood and went to get a book of poems by Wordsworth.

"Your favorite poet," Yannette told me when she read on the cover the author's name.

I smiled and said, "Do you remember that our father liked to read poems about nature?"

"Yes, especially Wordsworth's Prelude. As Wordsworth, my father preferred the country," Yannette said.

Then, we had an appetite and went to dinner in the main dining room of the house.

The next day, the sound of crickets woke me up. For a while, I stayed in bed. Then I went to the library, I sat behind a desk and wrote a few chapters for my novel. Later, I stood and looked at the garden through the window. As I looked around, I remembered my father. I thought that I had not seen him for years. I wanted to return to Chile to establish myself with a university and educate as many people as I could. That day, my father existed only in the world of ideas or memories and not the senses.

For a while I wrote again. That morning, I had breakfast with the rest of my family. Then we went for a walk in the countryside. The day was beautiful. The sun was shining everywhere, warming the morning, but it was still cold.

"How beautiful is the day!" I said.

As we walked, the dogs wagged their tails at our side. Some of them ran while others stretched their legs.

A worker greeted us with his cap in his hand, and my brother Hugo asked,

"How's work?"

"Very good, sir," the worker said.

He was the gardener who was trimming the trees. The grapevines had already been pruned. That day, we wore jackets, woolen sweaters, pants, and boots. The clothes became wet with morning dew when we got to an area of the farm with no footpath, but we just made our way through the bushes. Then, we came out to a grove overlooking the road. Water drops on green leaves of the trees shone like diamonds.

"Be careful . . . the roadway has many fallen branches," my older brother Hugo said when we left the forest. The bird calls in the tall trees produced a delightful echo. Ahead, there was a stream. We stopped in front of it. I felt excited and walked to the water. "Oh, it's freezing!" I said when I touched the water. In the summer, we swam in the river that had tall lindens, oaks, and cypress trees that overhung the river covered with leaves, so the water was cold all of the time.

"We should return," Yannette said.

From time to time, we heard the buzzing of bees, as we smelled the chamomile, mint and lemon balm. The dried leaves sounded like crackling paper when we stepped on them. The mud stuck to our shoes. The soft breeze moved the leaves and vines dotted with bluebells.

"Walk carefully," Hugo said.

With family and workers, we used to go out for walks in the countryside when we were kids.

"Don't worry," some of us said.

For a while we sat on a log and looked around. Later, a partridge came out of the bushes on the right and we screamed and jumped with fright. But then we started to laugh.

"We should go back," I said.

When we were near the house, my mom went to a balcony and said,

"Hello children."

We waved and she stood there for a while. Some workers drew open the curtains and cleaned the glass in the windows.

Back at home, we tried to open the bedroom windows that had not been opened for some time. As we did it, sunshine came in. Then, we had lunch and then enjoyed talking. So, in that way night came.

CHAPTER XIX

That night, after dinner, we talked for some time in the living room. Then, I went upstairs to the library and the rest of the family stayed there watching television. The children had gone to bed earlier than the adults. In the library, I felt the silence as I sat at my desk and wrote new chapters for my novel. I went to bed quietly. I did not want to wake the others. In bed, I smiled as I thought of Pierre for a while. I had not seen him for some days, but I missed him. Then, I imagined how it would be if I had a kindergarten in Chile. A while later, I fell asleep and dreamed that I built a university in Yungay. In the dream, it was Christmas time and I had an English daughter. The English had helped me build the university. Next to a big Christmas tree at my university, called "Cambridge of Chile," I saw myself surrounded by children while reporters interviewed me on how I felt about being in my country after so many years. I hugged the children and told them that my greatest satisfaction was to have built my university. The university building had four floors and from each classroom hung a chandelier that looked like diamonds. The fourth floor was a large library with shelves filled with books. My passion was to teach anyone who wanted to learn.

When I awoke, I smiled, thinking about the dream. Then, I turned on the light and went to the library to write more chapters for my novel. First, I skimmed through what I had written. While reading, I thought that degrees in psychology and journalism would be one of the most important ones. I tried to read the manuscript, but the idea of having my own university did not allow me to concentrate on reading the manuscript. I could not put away the thought of having a university. For a long time, I looked out of the window. It was dark outside. I heard many birds moving and tweeting in the branches of the chestnut trees. That morning there was a soft breeze moving the leaves of the chestnut and other trees. After a while, I heard a sound like tapping. I walked over to see what the sound was, but there was nobody. I went back to the window and continued looking out. All of a sudden, I jumped and screamed horrified when I saw someone standing by the door because I thought it was a ghost. It was a worker with a kerosene lamp.

"What are you doing here, Miss, Victoria?" a worker asked.

"Oh, my God, you scared me!" I said.

"Miss, sorry it was not my intention to scare you," the worker said shrugging his shoulders.

"All right," I said.

"Do you want some coffee, miss," the worker asked.

"No, thanks."

"Why don't you go to bed, miss?" he asked me.

"No yet, but you go to bed."

The worker left the library. Hearing my scream, some of my brothers got up and ran to the library to find out what had happened. After I told them what had happened, we went to bed.

The next morning, after breakfast we walked through the garden.

Smiling I said, "I remember once when I was with a boyfriend here, I noticed that someone was moving the branches of a tree. When I looked up, I saw a frightened worker looking at us perched on a branch. Then, he asked me to excuse him as he crawled down the chestnut tree. I told him that it was okay for that time, but he should not repeat it again."

"It must have been Gaston because he was very nosy," Yannette said.

"Yes, he was like a curious bird," I said.

We smiled as we talked about my experience. It was in the summer, under a blue sky covered with stars. The workers used to climb the trees and watched us from above.

Then we walked to the pool and sat on chaise lounges. After talking for a while, I laid down and fell asleep.

I woke when I heard the voice of Karincita's children playing in the yard. My niece Karincita had gone to the bedroom to get a sweater for them.

Later, we returned for lunch. As we ate, we talked of the past. We remembered when we went to see the rodeo. Then, one of my brothers came to the table and continued eating with us.

"What shall we do this weekend?" my brother asked.

"Why don't we go to the rodeo that will be this weekend?"

I said smiling.

"Let's go," my brother Robert said.

"Yes, of course!" I said enthusiastically.

We decided to go to the rodeo. I could not wait to see a rodeo after so many years.

CHAPTER XX

On **Saturday of** that weekend in Yungay, my family and I anticipated having fun at the rodeo. Happily, we reached the rodeo at about one o'clock. But, unexpectedly, it began to rain and the rodeo was postponed for another day. We returned to the house for lunch.

The next day, back at the rodeo, we looked around. It was more interesting than we expected. We could hear the music of the *cuecas*, which is the traditional Chilean dance, played by the Brothers Campos, which was a popular group at the rodeos. Many couples were dressed in colorful clothes walking with their children to sit in the stands. Men on horses herded young bulls in the rodeo grounds next to the stands. A wooden fence enclosed the rodeo grounds. Inside we saw the riders on horseback. *Huasos*, Chilean cowboys were dressed with their straw hats, colorful ponchos, and tight pants into boots with spurs. The *huasos*, controlling the reins of the horses trotted into the rodeo grounds while a wild and restless bull ran around the corral. Meanwhile, people waited anxiously for the rodeo to start. The sizzling *empanadas* that some women were frying in fireplaces, made us hungry.

The training of the wild and young bulls by Chilean *huasos* was very dear to my father. He liked going to rodeos.

After a while, the rodeo began. From the stands, people cheered the riders when they made their appearance. They started the rodeo running after the wild bulls. They sped and stopped pulling back the reins making the horses rear up on their hind legs. The bulls were frightened and almost ran over the fence but then turned and were cornered by the horsemen. Some riders were able to corner the bulls against the area marked to get points, which the announcer blared through the loudspeakers. Some people clapped and cheered enthusiastically while others stood up and raised both arms shouting to the winners, "Bravo!" Others had no such luck and the bulls returned and the riders got no points.

Vendors walked through the stands with their baskets full of *empanadas* and drinks. Some people shouted, "Over here! We want some." So we also bought *empanadas* and cokes and ate and drank them while watching the rodeo.

"The *empanadas* taste almost like homemade," my mother said.

"Yes, they are very delicious," Carmen said.

The people cheered when the riders rode behind the bulls and suddenly pulled the reins of their horses and they reared up on two legs trapping the bulls against the fence and scoring points. The audience applauded when the *huasos* were in control of their horses to tame the bulls. In that way, we enjoyed the rodeo. When it ended, people who attended came down from the stands, crowding and jostling one another. In the yard, the riders dismounted from their horses, sat on benches, and toasted with glasses of red wine. Other men dressed as *huasos*, took off the saddles and let the horses graze in a nearby pasture.

That day, as it was a little cold, we had a glass of wine at a table where they sold *empanadas*. Then, we got into the Range Rover and went home.

That evening, we ate chestnuts and talked enthusiastically about the rodeo and other things. Then, we had a delicious soup and then went to bed. But I went to the library and sat behind the desk to write more chapters for my novel. The house had many dogs that barked at night. When I had written a few pages, my sister went to get a law book from the library.

We talked for a while. As she gave me some ideas to put in the novel, she said there was fresh cow's milk from the country and went to the kitchen and brought a jug of cow's milk on a tray. She and I drank a glass of milk quickly. Then I asked her for another glass. My sister had brought a jug because she knew that I was used to drinking more than a glass of milk.

Then, we went to bed and while I slept, I dreamt that we were in the big house in Yungay. It was summer in the dream, our family walked through a field of wheat swaying in the breeze. The sky was blue without any clouds. The dew wet our clothing as we made a path across through the wheat straw in the morning. The dew on the golden wheat straw looked like crystals. Later, the sun was shining and dried the wheat straws. The dry wheat crackled as we passed through them.

"The wheat is very good!" my father said when he took some wheat and rubbed it in his hands.

"The wheat harvest will be very good," one of my brothers said.

The wheat grains were full and large. We laughed when we looked at the partridges running out of their nests and suddenly undertook a low flight and some of their feathers floated in the air. Other times, the partridges sat on their nests among the wheat and the chicks chirped when they peeked out of the edge of their nests.

Later in the dream, there were wild cherry trees. In the shade of one of them that was filled with cherries, we sat on wheat straws. Then we picked some cherries to eat. They were sweet. In the distance we heard the voices of the workers. It was time for breakfast. The juice of sour cherries cooled and satisfied us. Then, one after another, we stood and continued opening our way among the wheat straws. The chirping birds filled us with great joy. After walking a while, we arrived at the top of the hill and we looked across at the countryside. All of a sudden, a worker of our farm appeared holding the hand of a little boy and ran to greet us. Then, all the other workers followed.

"Hello, hello!" they said.

"Hello, how are you?" we said.

The children jumped up and down in pure joy of seeing us.

Then, as we walked toward the huge front entrance, the garden gate opened and we realized it was a castle. A princess was walking with her dog in the garden. She welcomed us happily. Suddenly, it began to rain in torrents and we ran through the rain inside the castle while listening to the raindrops on the leaves of the trees.

The next morning, I woke up to the sound of the conversations of the farm workers who were sweeping the leaves in the yard. The sun had not risen yet. For a while, I lay in bed thinking about the dream. The more I thought about it, the more I thought about the summertime when we got up at sunrise to go for walks through the wheat and my father read fairy tales to us.

Then, I stood and went to the balcony and looked out. The breeze shook my pink pajamas. It had drizzled and was still cloudy. Afterwards, I went to the library and sat behind the desk to write more chapters for the novel. When I had written for an hour, I looked out the window as the sun entered.

CHAPTER XXI

That morning, I was happy to be in Yungay after living abroad for so many years even though I felt the absence of my father. Autumn had the country covered with leaves and the birds were chirping everywhere. For a while, I remembered my happy childhood. Later, I went to my bedroom and then took a bath.

As I bathed, I thought of Pierre and many other things, "What is he doing? Does he think of me? How would it had been if he had come to spend the vacation with us? Would he remember that day when we went to the municipal theater and he tried to kiss me?" Then, when I heard footsteps of someone in the hallway, I stood, and put on blue jeans, a shirt, a sweater, and boots.

Then, I went to have breakfast with my family in the dining room on the first floor, but when I heard conversations in the kitchen, I went there. They were warming themselves around a fireplace.

"Did you sleep well, Victoria?" my mom asked.

"Yes, Mom, thank you, and you?"

They said they had slept really well.

"Mom, I want to eat *soplillo* and *guatongo*," I said.

"Victoria, the *soplillo* is made in the summer with unripe wheat," my brother Robert said.

"Oh, really?" I said.

"Victoria, in the summer when you come, we're going to prepare all your favorite foods," Hugo said.

"Okay," I said with a warm smile.

They had not eaten *soplillo* for a long time, but I inspired them to eat it this summer. The maids knew how to prepare all the traditional foods of the summer season. Sometimes, the kitchen was filled with people preparing *humas* or *empanadas*. We all loved those meals.

While some of the workers went to get the wood they had cut the day before, others prepared breakfast.

The adults were around the fireplace while the kids jumped around laughing. Sometimes British pop music played on the radio.

"Here, we stood around the fireplace when we used to come with our dad," Yannette said.

"He never forgot the traditions," Hugo said.

"Yes, children," my mother said. "Your father was very traditional."

"Yes," I agreed.

Years ago, at the days of the Saints of some relatives, we cooked stews on the fireplace in clay pots. Through a slit in the back wall of the kitchen, we looked and listened to the foliage of the chestnut trees. Birds flitted among the branches. Suddenly, a loud noise startled us. It was some workers who suddenly dropped firewood next to us. We shouted and jumped frightened.

But then, we laughed, "Ha, ha, ha!" while the workers apologized. They never thought they were going to scare us.

"There is a lot of wood," one of the workers said brushing his hands on his sweater.

"Very well, Ruben," my mom said.

"Thank you, ma'am," the worker said.

From time to time, workers hugged their children as they played around. That morning the sun shone. Before breakfast, we went for a walk. To the right, we saw a beehive. Bees were flying in and out of the boxes. The bees buzzed as they flew to the flowers that were near the apiary.

"Don't touch the bees," I said to a child of a worker, who leaned over to touch them.

"Hey, Victoria!" my mother said. "They know how to touch them."

"Yes," Yannette agreed.

"My boy grabs pieces of wax with honey and eats them and the bees don't do anything to him," the worker said.

"Amazing!" I said.

As some bees flew around some plums that had fallen during the summer, a worker said,

"In the summer many plums fell and they're still good for the bees."

I felt a lot of excitement to look at all that.

To the left, we could see the river surrounded by trees. It watered the crops in the spring. Then, we walked around the yard under a grape trellis. When we passed the stable, we smelled manure coming from it. Later, we went across to the river. We walked along it for a while until we came to where there once was a windmill. There, we sat on a log under a plum tree that still had some plums. We listened to the thrushes flying from branch to branch in the trees.

Across the river grew patches of chamomile where we used to roll over when we were children. In the summer, we smelled the aroma of the herbs when we went through the driveway to the house.

That day, the workers were cutting firewood. They put the wood in piles and hauled them on a tractor to a storage shed. Many leaves could be seen floating in the river. In the spring, we loved watching the ducks swimming there with their young.

"Do you still like the farm, Victoria?" my mom asked.

"I love it!"

A warm breeze shook the leaves of the trees while we heard the bleating of the sheep and the bellowing of cows.

That day we wore boots, pants, and parkas with hoods.

"How beautiful!" I said looking around.

When breakfast was prepared, a worker went to tell us and my mom said, "Let's go to have breakfast!"

On the first floor dining room, we sat at the table. That morning, I found the steaming cow's milk very tasty. We all drank milk with toasted homemade bread with peach marmalade. It was cold outside, but the warmth of the fireplace heated inside.

On the radio, a Beatle's song began to play and I turned up the volume. I liked their songs. My niece Katy started singing the song. She had learned it at Mary Immaculate School. She pronounced the words with a British accent. When the song ended, Katherine said,

"At school, we're studying the conjugation of verbs."

"It's very important to know them," I said.

"Here you have Auntie Victoria to teach you English," my mother said.

"Yes, of course!" I said.

"Victoria is an English teacher," Yannette said.

"And also a teacher of English literature," I said.

Then, the radio played another song of John Lennon, "Woman." I could not contain my tears. I thought of an English boyfriend who was very important in my life. When we finished breakfast, we stood and went out for a walk. Outside the sun was shining as never before. That day, we agreed to go horseback riding the next morning.

CHAPTER XXII

The next day at dawn, we were excited to go horseback riding. It was foggy, but little by Little it cleared. At home, we had English horses. My father said they were the best. After we mounted the horses, we started the ride. The dogs barked at our sides and brushed one another happily, wagging their tails.

Later in the wheat field, we laughed while we trotted by the wheat field that had been harvested in the summer. The sun shone on our faces while the dogs ran by our side. We were very good at horseback riding.

While we trotted, the feathers of the partridges flew out when they ran trying to fly from their nests in the straws of wheat.

"My dad taught Katy and Yosi to ride," Yannette said.

I looked at her daughters and said, "I can see that."

Suddenly, the horses stood on two legs when we threw back the reins.

"Ha-ha-ha," we laughed.

"We should not laugh like that. If anyone heard us, they would say that we're not in mourning for our father," I said.

"Victoria, our father must be happy that their children can go horseback riding in his estate. In that way we follow his tradition that he loved so much," one of my sisters said.

Minutes later, my brother Hugo shot a hare with a rifle and the sheep and cows that were grazing around panicked and ran in all directions. Then, all of a sudden, Israel, a worker came running and said,

"Do you want me to pick up the rabbit and take it home and cook it?"

"Oh, yes. And make a stew!"

"Yes, sir. These are very tasty and scrumptious that makes one want to suck one's fingers!"

The worker left with the hare on his shoulder and we then broke out laughing, for he was one of the funniest workers.

As we continued riding, we compared the present with the past. All the houses in the town and the farm of my parents were well maintained.

Afterward, when we saw the house of an aunt, we realized that it was abandoned. The house looked as if it had not been painted for years. We dismounted to look at the house. The white paint on the rectangular building was peeling. In the garden, the flowers climbed on the trees, iron fences, and concrete walls. The structure of the house still looked good, but needed repairs and a complete renovation.

After much struggling, we opened the front door. Dust blew in the air when we tried to open the windows. Excitedly, we toured the mansion with great curiosity. We could tell it had not been cleaned for a long time. When we opened a few windows, dust rose from the drapes at the windows and the beige sofas. We remembered how we used to dance the tango with our cousins. Then, we went to the dining room. Some family portraits still hung in the dining room. The dust on the marble floor looked like sand. After some time, we went upstairs. The bedrooms were dark, but when we opened the windows of some of them, the sunlight came in and lit the rooms. From the balcony, we looked out. We smelled manure coming from the pasture. Several horses and cows were grazing around the mansion.

After opening almost every window of the 20 rooms of the mansion, the air smelled of dust and manure.

Then, we went to the cellar. There, we found cognac and took a bottle that was dusty. From a cabinet, we took out some glasses. We cleaned them with the sleeve of our sweaters and tried it.

"It's very good and it has a clear and rich amber color," one of my brothers said.

Another brought his nose close to the glass and said, "It smells like spice scents."

"Yes, it's has a spicy and a nutty smell and flavor," I said.

"We would enjoy the cognac more if we mix it with chocolate or lemon," one of my brothers said.

After a while, we left the cellar and went to the balcony. As we walked down the hallway, we saw many dusty portraits on the walls. We cleaned them and saw the portraits of the family on the farm. I could not believe that such a beautiful country mansion was neglected.

"We have to clean the house," I said.

We agreed to send some of our housemaids to clean our aunt's mansion.

"The maintenance of this house must be expensive," one of my brothers said.

"Yes of course," I said.

Thinking and wondering why the children of my aunt had abandoned the mansion, I saw something on the wall that looked like dusty paintings. But, we realized that they were family portraits when we removed the dust.

As I walked out of the cellar with bottles of wine and cognac, I thought of making wine again, as a family business. Our family was one of the first who had vineyards in Chile. We were the first to make and sell wine and cognac in Chile. But wine was against my passion for all things having to do with learning because many youths could become addicted to alcohol and abandon their studies.

The dogs ran ahead of us, while the warm breeze swayed the foliage of trees and grasses. On the top of the branches of some trees, there were red *copihues*, which are wild vines with red flowers like large bells that grow only in Chile. The sky was blue. Later, we looked at a stream overhung with the branches of trees.

"It looks very refreshing!" I said.

We decided to go there. We stopped in front of it and the horses drank water. We talked for a while looking across the stream.

"Let's go," Hugo said and pulled the reins of his horse.

We all pulled the reins and continued riding along the creek. We rode next to each other talking and enjoying the ride. Suddenly, a rabbit crossed our path and we laughed.

"Look, look!" I shouted.

"It's the rabbit that escaped from the pot of Israel," Hugo joked.

We laughed.

We rode through the middle of the farm covered with wheat straw. In January, they had harvested the wheat. The straws were yellow.

"Here we used to come with my father," Yannette said.

"But, he was fine at that time," I asked.

"Yes, Victoria," Hugo said. Many times he put the sacks of wheat in the truck.

For a while, we rode through the wheat field. The horses whinnied while our hair flew back.

"Victoria, do you remember, Charles, the Englishman?"

"Yes, why wouldn't I remember him," I interrupted. "Why?"

"He wants us to establish a Polo Club," Yannette said.

"It would be great to have a Polo Club," I said.

"Charles is abroad," Yannette, whom we called Yani said.

"When is he coming back?" I asked.

"I think one of these days," one of my brothers said.

"Charles grew up as a brother with us, so how am I not going to remember him," I said.

"He was in love with you, remember?" Yannette said smiling.

"I don't think so! Is he still single?" I said.

"Yes, and handsome as ever," Yannette said.

The Englishman had taught them to play polo like in England. My father loved everything that was English, as he was of English descent. Then we continued talking about the idea of the polo club.

"It's a great idea," I replied.

"My dad also thought that it was a good idea," Yannette

replied.

Charles felt at home in ours. Here Polo was a sport that was virtually unknown, but Charles had familiarized us with that aristocratic sport.

"The English horses are the best," my father often said, as we were taught to ride those horses.

Then, we returned to the house. For a while, it drizzled. But then the deep blue sky became clear again. We entered the driveway and headed home. Riding the horses, we passed the fruit orchard. There were still apples on the trees. We picked some, cleaned them, and ate them. We continued heading to the mansion. Workers smiled when they saw us coming. Some of them greeted us warmly.

"My mom says that here stood the barons, which were the wooden barriers which were raised to enter after approval of the owner," Yannette said as we approached the entrance to the courtyard.

"Every time I read a romance novel of the Middle Ages, I remember this country estate," I said.

"Why?" Yannette asked.

"Because in medieval literature, there is the huge mansion or castle of the king and queen surrounded by knights and barons who depend on the king. As in medieval romances, this mansion has many workers who depend on the patron. Besides, there is a garden with a fountain in the middle like in the medieval romances," I said.

"Also, the tradition of the rich country estate and in literature maintains the extravagance and gallantry of good manners," Yannette said.

"I love the gallantry of the knights of the Middle Ages," I added as we rode. "But as in the Middle Ages, now, there isn't a lord protector of the chivalric order."

"But the courteous ideals continued in the family," Hugo said.

In the courtyard, the workers were sweeping the leaves fallen from the trees.

That morning, the hours passed quickly.

"Good afternoon, happy to serve you," one of the funniest workers, who was missing some teeth, said.

We greeted him, and other workers came to meet us to help us dismount.

"These are very good horses," the worker said.

"Yes," one of my brothers said.

My father enjoyed the conversation with his workers, who were very faithful to him.

"Are you going to start pruning the vines," I asked one of them.

"No yet, miss."

"When will you start?" I asked.

The worker smiled and said, "One of these days, miss."

"The rose bushes don't have roses," Yannette said.

"They fell with the rain," the worker said kindly.

Another worker, who took the saddle off a horse, interrupted his work and said smiling to the horse, "How did you behave with the rider?"

We left them working and walked across the yard to the house.

"What's for lunch?" I asked one of the workers.

"A delicious rabbit stew," she answered.

"One of my favorite foods," I said.

After we showered, we went to the table for lunch. This was covered with a white flowered tablecloth and white napkins. In the middle of it, there was a basket full of tortillas and two bottles of wine that were unopened.

We had stew with tomatoes and lettuce salad. While we talked, the maids served the food.

"Children, how was your ride?" my mom asked.

"Great," we said almost in chorus.

We remembered other times when we went out hunting, and then talked about other things.

"When are you going to get married Robert?" I asked.

He smiled and said, "I don't know, Victoria!"

"He's liked by many women," my mother said.

"Sometimes, women fight for his affection," Yannette said, "So, sometimes I have to defend him."

Robert was not a great seducer, but women saw him as a good match, handsome, gallant, and well educated and they fought to get his love.

"Once two women fought over him," my mother said.

The garden that was seen through the window looked well maintained as before. Sometimes, we heard the workers chatting in the yard.

That day, Pierre had called me while we were riding. He was yearning to speak to me. He had gotten used to seeing me almost every day. While I enjoyed my vacation with my family, I thought about Pierre occasionally. During the days he did not see me, his love for me grew stronger and stronger. In the afternoons, when he drove from work to his house, he played a song we had heard together over and over.

"It's our song," he smiled as he heard it and saw himself with me in his imagination.

He was in love with me and thought I was too. He called me almost every day. When he thought that I could find another man, he become very jealous.

In the evening, we went upstairs to the living room and sat on sofas eating almonds. We remembered how we used to pile books in the library and step on them to get books that were high on bookshelves.

"All of you have loved books since a very early age," my mom said.

"That's why I become a writer," I said.

We were delighted to talk about the past. Then, at night, we had dinner in the main dining room. That day, there was chicken soup for dinner.

CHAPTER XXIII

The following day, there was a bright sunshine and the sky was blue, but it was cold. That day we had spaghetti with filet mignon and tomato salad for lunch and strawberries with cream for dessert. As we ate, we heard the sound of a vehicle coming up the driveway.

My mom went to look out of the window.

"It's your granddaughter Karincita," a worker who was walking through the courtyard said.

My mom smiled and hurried to greet them. Then, we all followed. Outside, Karincita and her husband Edward and their children were coming up the driveway. I was happy to see them. Moments later, the vehicle stopped in the yard. Edward got out first and then opened the door for Karincita and his two children. The children ran to my mother's arms. "Hi, Monchi, Mati," my mom kissed and hugged them. We greeted each other warmly and then walked into the kitchen chatting while the children ran in front of us screaming happily to the kitchen.

"It was a long journey!" Karincita said with a warm smile.

"We're very happy to have you here," my mom said kissing and embracing her granddaughter.

The children ran here and there with excitement.

"Don't shout so loud, dear!" Karincita said to her son Mati.

"Yes, Mom," Mati said laughing.

"I'm not screaming, Mom," Monchi said.

"No, my dear," Karincita said and took her in her arms.

"Ha, ha!" Mati laughed when he embraced the dogs that came to greet them playing and wagging their tails.

When we entered the kitchen, Monchi smelled food and said, "I'm hungry, mom."

"Wait a minute, my dear," Karincita said.

My mom smiled and hugged her great-granddaughter Monchi. It was a long time since I had not met my family in the country estate of Yungay.

"Nana," my mom said to one of the maids.

"Yes, ma'am," the Nana said.

"Serve lunch to the children and their parents," my mother said.

"Yes, ma'am," the Nana said. "Do I serve them chocolate with peaches for dessert?"

"Yes," my mother said.

Karincita, her husband, and the children sat at the table next to us and continued having lunch with us.

"The spaghetti is delicious," Karincita said.

"This spaghetti is very different from the Italian one," I said.

"Oh, the Italian spaghetti has too much cheese," one of

my sister said.

"What's that, Mama?" Mati said, showing a bottle of wine.

"Wine, dear," Karincita said.

"Can I drink a bit, Mom?" Mati asked.

"No, honey! Kids don't drink wine," Karincita said.

A maid approached the table and filled two glasses of Coca-Cola for Monchi and Mati. The children thanked her and drank it all, as they were thirsty.

"Do you like the spaghetti?" my mother asked.

"Yes," Mati said playing with the spaghetti in his plate. He had never done this behavior before, but this time he was very happy to see us all there.

"It's good!" Montserrat said.

One of the maids pulled out the corks of the bottles of red wine, and then filled the glasses and we toasted touching raised glasses.

"It has strawberry flavor," Hugo said.

"Yes, it's very good," Yannette said.

The children ate very fast. When Mati finished eating, he said, "It was very delicious."

"Do you want more?" a maid asked.

"Yes, please," Mati said happily.

The maid returned to fill the plates of the two children.

During the afternoon we walked and talked of many things. With excitement, we spoke about what we had done during the time that we did not see one another. In the garden, we laughed when the children ran screaming after a rabbit. After a while, they got the rabbit and petted him.

That evening, after a snack of *empanadas*, I went to the library to get the manuscript of my novel. When I returned, some of my brothers and sisters had already left the table.

But they went back when I told them to read my novel. All of us read a part of it. When my brother Hugo began to read, tears rolled down his cheeks and our eyes watered. Then my mother began to read it. In that way, the ones who were sitting read. Robert had gone to the yard to get persimmons. When he came back and stood beside my mother, he took the book and continued reading. We looked at him as he read.

Robert, whom we called Titin, graciously said, "Let's applaud…" after he read a scene where I was signing autographs. We smiled when he said that graciously. He looked at us fascinated. Robert read very well. At times, Hugo's daughter corrected the grammar while reading. She was a teacher of Spanish literature. A cousin who had a bakery also read. She had brought us empanadas. As we read, we smelled the scent of empanadas.

Later, we bathed the children and then took them to have dinner and then to bed. They were tired and fell asleep quickly. Then, the adults had dinner.

"Karincita, when are you traveling to Australia?" I asked.

"These days, auntie Victoria," she said.

"You could pass by Hawaii to see me," I said.

"Thanks auntie, maybe I'll stop in Hawaii when I go to Australia again," Karincita said.

After Hugo drank a few glasses of wine, he shared his experience in the Falklands War. Hugo said that he had arrived in the islands a day after the war was over and got drunk with the English officers who were celebrating the victory. The British officers were happy to share with the Chilean officers to whom they regarded as allies.

A while later, I decided to go to bed. The next day, I had to get up early to return to Santiago.

"Good night to all," I said.

"Why so early?" Yannette asked.

'Tomorrow, I have a meeting with the editor of my novel," I replied.

"Share with us a little more," my mother said.

"I'd like to, but I have to be in Santiago very early tomorrow," I answered.

"I'll drive," Yannette said.

"Yes, but I have a commitment tomorrow," I insisted.

"Stay a little longer," Hugo said.

"I cannot," I replied.

"All right," Hugo said.

I stood at the table and walked to my bedroom, which was next to the children's. While I tried to sleep, the noise that was coming from the dining room would not let me sleep until everyone went to bed.

CHAPTER XXIV

The next day, my brothers, sisters, nieces, my mom, and I got up at five in the morning. After I dressed, I had breakfast with the ones who were returning to Santiago and then walked to the Range Rover.

"Good morning, Miss," one of the workers, who was busy putting the bags in the vehicle, said.

"Good morning, it's a little cold!" I said.

It was still dark and drizzling outside. Inside, the fireplace in the living room warmed the house. The leaves of the trees were wet with rain.

The others were left sleeping. Some workers had already gotten up. After we said, "Good bye," we got in the Range Rover and started our trip to Santiago.

"We're leaving," I said to a worker who was walking in the driveway.

"Have a wonderful trip!" the worker said to us.

"Thanks," my mother said.

When we came out of the driveway, we turned right. Some trees along both sides of the road still had some green leaves among the dry leaves.

About an hour later, the fields were covered with wheat straw, with cows, and sheep grazing. Along the way, we saw many country people who were riding on horseback. They greeted us with a bow taking off their hats.

Later, when I looked at the clock, I said, "We must hurry."

"Yes, I know," Hugo said.

"Don't worry. We'll arrive very early in Santiago," my mother said.

"Yes, but it's already a little late," I replied.

In the Range Rover, the heating warmed the interior of the vehicle. Smoke was coming out from some chimneys. Later, the sun started to come out. Occasionally, there was a smell of fried onions and toast. It was early. It seemed that people were having breakfast. We left behind the large houses surrounded by countryside. Before arriving to Chillán, the sun shone. In the city, we saw many groups of teenagers, boys and girls, wearing school uniforms walking on both sides of the street.

"In that way, I would like students to read my novel," I said when I saw one with a book in hand.

"Don't worry, it will be a success," Yannette said.

I smiled when I imagined those young students reading my novel. Some of them looked at us and smiled. The Range Rover attracted people's attention because it was a new brand in Chile. We passed several towns where all the houses looked the same.

"What time do you have to see the editor?" Yannette asked.

"At ten o'clock."

"I thought it was later," Hugo said.

"Oh no!" I said.

Then, we entered downtown Chillán. We passed through the bus terminal that went to Yungay. There were many people coming in and out of the place. I saw several buses that were, at that time, full of passengers. Many people walked with bags and suitcases in their hands.

Next, we passed by Chillán market where we saw through open doors many people eating. Other people sold fruits and vegetables in front of their stalls. We saw that in one, people sold mote, which is peeled green wheat. We decided to buy mote with peach juice. Yannette's daughters rushed to buy them. Then when they got back, we looked around as we ate.

"It tastes very good," I said.

"It's been many years since you had not eaten mote with fruits," my mother said.

"Yes, but I remembered the taste," I said.

"The mote with peach juice is very refreshing," Yannette said.

' "Yes," Titin said.

After our quick stop at the market in Chillán, the vehicle entered the freeway. I must admit I would have liked to get out of the vehicle at the Chillán market to buy some handmade things, but then I thought it was better to wait and buy them in Santiago.

The Range Rover was going about 100 mph on the highway.

"Don't worry. We'll arrive on time," Hugo said.

I thought of calling the editor, but luckily he called me first.

"Hello, how are you, Victoria?" I heard him saying.

"Fine, thanks and you?" I said.

"Okay, thank you. I called to ask you to get together this afternoon or on Wednesday to discuss the book because I have a problem this morning."

"Don Françoise, I'm coming back to Santiago. I'm near Talca, so I prefer to get together on Wednesday. Please tell me what time."

We agreed to get together next Wednesday at ten o'clock at Coffee Tabelli in Manuel Montt. I always liked to do the important things early.

"What happened?" Yannette asked.

"It's not necessary to go so fast. The editor and I decided to meet on Wednesday," I said.

"Good!" Yannette replied enthusiastically.

"I hope to publish the novel soon," I said.

About an hour later, I turned up the volume of the radio to hear better a song I liked. As I listened and looked at the countryside, I thought that my novel could be translated into different languages.

Hours later, we arrived in Santiago, and we left the freeway and entered the narrow streets.

Some students were walking on the sidewalks. Some walked fast and others slow. Others were windows shopping. I thought I was fortunate that the editor had called me to see me this afternoon or Wednesday to discuss my book.

Later, the Range Rover took the Alameda to get to Las Condes. We noticed a lot of traffic despite the hour. Some people were waiting for the Transantiago buses, which were late most of the time.

As we passed in front of the Paseo Ahumada Boulevard, it

looked like a real beehive of people walking in all directions. Classical music was heard from the boulevard

After we passed through Providencia, we finally arrived in Las Condes. The Range Rover stopped in front of the house.

Back in the house, as usual, the workers came to greet us. There was not so much smog in the air. We got out of the vehicle and walked to the front door of the mansion.

The workers took the bags out of the vehicle. One was cleaning the windows on the second floor. Another of the workers opened the front door, and we entered.

"Good morning, how was the trip?" one of the workers asked.

"Very good!" my mother said.

Some maids put the clothing in the closets. Others took the food from bags and put them in the refrigerator. That morning was beautiful. Mom found that some rooms smelled musty.

"Open the windows," my mother said to some workers.

"Yes, ma'am," some of them answered.

Then, one after another, the maids began to open them.

CHAPTER XXV

That day at night, in Santiago, we grilled *longanizas*, which is a type of sausage made of pork and spices. We stood around the grilling under the grape trellises. While the sausages sizzled, we picked up some small pieces and ate them with contentment.

"They're delicious!" I said smiling.

"Very good!" Carmen said.

"You have always liked the sausages made in the country," my mother said.

"Yes, of course. They're very good," Yannette said.

That night, the sky was starry. We were with woolen coats. It was cold.

The workers walked around. Then, we sat at the dinner table and ate grilled sausages with tomato salad and homemade bread that we had brought from the farm in the south. Hugo opened a bottle of red wine. He filled the glasses with wine and toasted to the harmony of the family, clinking the glasses.

Often a maid came looking around if we needed anything. Then, they served dessert.

"Put chocolate on the fresh strawberries," my mother told the maid who had forgotten to do it.

"Yes, ma'am," the maid said with a warm smile.

The dining room was warm by the heat of the fireplace, which was next to a large window facing the terrace.

"Tomorrow, I'd like to go to the library of the Catholic University," I said.

"There are many books there," Yannette replied.

"What kind of books are you going to look for?" Carmen asked.

"Cognitive psychology in Spanish," I said.

"How interesting!" Yannette said.

As we ate, Pierre called on the phone.

"Mr. Lovell is calling you, Miss Victoria," the maid said.

"Thanks," I said, taking the receiver.

"Hi, my love! How are you? How was the trip?" Pierre said excitedly.

"Fine, thanks, and you?"

"I missed you very much my love," Pierre murmured.

"Me too," I whispered lovingly.

"Can we meet tonight?" he asked.

"Tonight?"

"Yes, my love."

"Oh, no, I'm having dinner with my family."

"How about if we go to a restaurant tomorrow?" Pierre said.

"Tomorrow?" I asked.

"Yes," he replied.

Inside the house there were sounds of conversations and

dishes.

"I'd like to. . . but tomorrow I have to go to the Catholic University," I said.

"Why don't you go there another day?" Pierre asked.

"I cannot really," I replied.

"Let's meet tomorrow even if it is just for only a little while," Pierre asked me nervously.

"It would be better another day," I replied.

"Can I accompany you to the university?" Pierre asked anxiously.

"Well, all right," I said.

We agreed to get together the next afternoon in the psychology section of the library of the university.

"My love, I wished I was there to hug you and kiss you," he said romantically.

CHAPTER XXVI

Pierre arrived earlier than I at the university. He waited for me, sitting on a sofa in the psychology section. After a few minutes, he stood and began to leaf through volumes on perception and understanding. A while later, he started walking on the side of some shelves filled with books while he thought that he could not live without my love. Therefore, he did not mind waiting for me for hours, he could not wait to see me. Sometimes, when Pierre heard footsteps, he looked around thinking it was me.

When I arrived an hour later, Pierre ran to greet me with a loving kiss as he put his arms around my waist. I had never seen him so happy. His square jaws smelled of aftershave cologne. He had imagined kissing me again and again, but now it was real. He was next to me kissing me. He seemed thinner while I seemed to have gained weight eating all those things I had not eaten for years. He looked handsome with a soft brown leather jacket unbuttoned, a green sweater, white shirt, soft brown pants, and sport shoes. He had an extravagant air. I was wearing a white leather jacket, a white sweater, light brown pants, and light brown boots.

"My love you're here!" Pierre said.

"Hmmm, honey!"

"As a lover Romeo, I was waiting for my Juliet!" Pierre told me lovingly.

"My love, don't talk about Shakespeare's tragedy," I said.

"I felt heartbroken during the days I did not see you, so don't get angry with me, my love," Pierre said with a soft voice.

"I'm not angry."

"Did you miss me, darling?" he asked me rising his eyebrows with pleasure.

"No," I said teasing him.

"No, my darling!" he said holding me close to him because he knew that I missed him.

I was a little upset when Pierre remembered that tragedy because I wanted my love affair with him to end well. Pierre did not want to do anything that I disliked.

Smiling we walked beside some shelves with books on psychology. Pierre kissed me and told me he loved me when he realized there was no one nearby.

Then, I told Pierre to help me to find books on cognition and perception. We started to look for books and skimmed through them standing next to the shelves.

"Do you like the book?" Pierre asked me when I was fascinated reading one.

"Yes, it's very interesting."

"Did you know that I spent hours standing here?" Pierre said.

"But you're a journalist!" I said a little puzzled.

"Yes . . . but I was going to be a cognitive psychologist," Pierre said.

"What a coincidence!" I said, looking at him surprised.

"Yes, we both like cognitive psychology," Pierre said and kissed me.

We continued reading, sitting at a desk next to the shelves. Then, we took a break for a while and talked.

"You had better not fall in love with me," I said quietly.

"Why?" Pierre asked.

"In a few days I'll return to the United States."

"Don't say that my love," Pierre said. "But, we can still see each other."

"I don't think so," I said.

"Why do you reject me?" Pierre asked.

I was happy with Pierre, but I did not want to fall in love with him.

Pierre looked at me and told me that I fascinated him. At times, he felt a little embarrassed when he remembered some fantasies with me.

"Would you go to Hawaii to see me?" I asked.

"Yes, my love," Pierre assured me.

"What about your work?" I said.

"I would go as a foreign correspondent," Pierre said.

"Would you truly follow me there?" I asked.

"Yes, I had never fallen for any woman the way I have fallen in love with you," Pierre whispered to me. "I would do anything to be close to you."

Pierre kissed me when there were no students around. But when we heard some steps, we continued talking and reading.

For a while, we read in silence. Then, we went to sit at some desks next to large windows. The more I read, the more I wanted to learn. Then in a notebook, I took notes on theories supported with experimental studies on cognition. Hours later, we left the library and walked down a hallway with high ceilings and classic marble floors. Many teachers and students walked talking quietly. Some greeted us. We laughed when he tried to hold my hand as we walked down the hallway, but I took it away. In minutes, we left the university and walked holding hands toward a restaurant downtown. Outside, the sun was still shining, but it was very cold. When we had walked a few blocks, Pierre leaned over and whispered.

"I love you."

A few minutes later, we arrived at the Paseo Ahumada Boulevard. We made our way among crowds of people. It bothered me to see so many people walking in all directions, but I liked the classical music in the background.

Then, Pierre asked me, "Why are walking so fast, my love?"

I smiled and said, "Do you really think I'm walking fast?"

"Yes, my love."

We walked slower. Further ahead, he leaned over and kissed me again when we were near a kiosk that sold newspapers and magazines. At that time, I heard that someone had used a camera. I thought that someone had taken a picture of us.

"Let's go in the Restaurant Ritz to eat something," Pierre suggested.

"No thanks. They're waiting for me to dine at home."

"Why don't you call them and tell them that you're going

to have dinner with me."

"I'd like to, but they prepared one of my favorite foods," I said.

"My love, let's go in even if it is just for a drink," Pierre insisted.

"Just for a juice," I said.

We crossed a few streets and then arrived at the Paseo Huerfanos Boulevard. Many people came and went in all directions. We passed in front of some restaurant windows that showed delicious meals. The food made me hungry. The trees, like the shower trees in Hawaii, on both sides of the boulevard, swayed in the cool breeze. There were benches to sit along both sides.

We kept walking while looking at the windows of restaurants and shops with clothing. We stopped in front of the Ritz and entered. A waiter guided us to a table near a large window.

We sat down and ordered juice. The table was set with an embroidered tablecloth and white napkins.

Minutes later, the waiter brought us the drinks in a tray and put them in front of each of us.

"Do you like it?" he asked.

"It's delicious," I replied as I sipped it.

Instrumental music was playing in the background. Through the window, we saw another kiosk with newspapers and magazines. Some people stopped and looked at the front pages of newspapers. Others sat on the benches to look around. After we drank the juice, we walked along the Paseo Huerfanos Boulevard. Suddenly, it began to drizzle. We stopped under a tree with huge foliage to protect us. Soon, it stopped raining, and we continued walking. Later, we ran over to a chocolate shop.

"Let's go in to buy chocolates!" Pierre said.

"Okay," I said.

Inside, we looked at the many boxes of chocolates.

"What chocolates do you like, honey?" Pierre asked me.

"The ones with walnuts," I replied.

"These are very good," I said, testing a sample of chocolate that was on a tray. "These chocolates had grapes, walnuts, and hazelnuts."

"They're very good," Pierre said.

Then, Pierre paid for them, and we left.

"Enjoy!" the saleswoman said smiling.

We left the chocolate shop and continued walking while eating chocolates. After we had walked for a while, it began to drizzle again and we hurried to take a taxi. Before we took it, Pierre embraced me. The rain fell on our faces. Pierre wiped the rain from my lips with kisses as I smiled. People passed by our side hurriedly, all with their umbrellas opened. Then, we stopped a taxi. Pierre opened the door for me to get in. Inside the vehicle, Pierre invited me to his house. I told him I could not and that it was better that the driver took us to each other's houses. During the ride, Pierre tried to kiss me again. But I twisted my face toward the window. The driver looked at us in the rear view mirror.

"Taxi drivers by habit are curious," I thought.

"Let's go to my house!" Pierre said again.

"I'd like to, Pierre, but I cannot."

"Why?"

"I have to go home to have dinner with my family and to correct the manuscript of my novel."

Within minutes, we reached the front of my house and

the driver stopped. Pierre got out first and opened the door for me. Then, we walked to the gate in front of my house. Almost at the entrance, Pierre hugged and kissed me.

"I love you," he told me.

I smiled and said, "I have to go."

"My love, don't go yet," he said holding my hand when I started walking towards the gate.

"Yes, I have to go."

"I love you, please understand me!" Pierre insisted.

He kissed me again, and we walked toward the gate. I opened it and entered. He looked at me from outside. That evening, there was a cool breeze. The windows of the house were closed and the curtains drawn. Inside, the lanterns in the garden in front of the house lit up the yard.

CHAPTER XXVII

Pierre went home. I found my family sitting at the table. I went to change my clothes and from the balcony of the second floor, I saw Pierre walking down the street. We kissed too long so the taxi left. Thinking how much he loved me, he took a taxi about five blocks away. The streets were empty. Then, it began to drizzle. Later, I went to dine with my family. As I did, I thought that Pierre must have felt rejected by me. Meanwhile, Pierre in the taxi decided to go for a drink to think about our romance. He told the taxi driver to stop outside a restaurant. As the drizzle turned into heavy rain, Pierre entered the restaurant. The lights of the restaurant shone through the large windows and reflected on the sidewalk. Pierre sat at a table next to a window. Soon, a waiter came to offer him something to drink.

"What do you want to drink, sir?" the waiter said.

"A whiskey, please," Pierre said.

While he waited, Pierre thought of me. When the waiter

brought the drink, Pierre drank it dry and ordered another.

"What's the matter, friend?" Asked a man who was looking from another table.

"The woman I love doesn't love me," Pierre said.

"That's an old story! Women are like that, we love them, but they don't love us," the man said to Pierre.

As he drank the second whiskey, Pierre thought how it would be if he were to marry me, but then he thought that I did not love him. Pierre was almost drunk when he paid for the whiskey and left the restaurant.

"Good luck with the woman you love, friend," Pierre overheard the man telling him.

Outside, Pierre took a taxi to get home.

Minutes later, he arrived home.

That night, Pierre hardly slept. He turned from side to side, thinking of me. He got up to get another glass of whiskey. The thought that I would return to the United States tormented him. Pierre was crazy in love with me.

That night, the rain beating down the windows did not let him sleep. Pierre got up and walked to the balcony. Outside, the rain shook the foliage while he was shivering.

He continued drinking whiskey at home looking out the window.

"I cannot bear the idea of not seeing her," he said distressed as tears streamed down his cheeks.

The leaves of the trees were shaking in the windy night. Other leaves were floating in the pool behind the house. Pierre smiled when he imagined that he and I swam playfully. The whiskey made him hallucinate with me.

Totally drunk, he fell asleep fully clothed on his bed. The next day, the sound of crickets woke him up. That day, he had to give the news on the evening news. Despite having a hangover that morning, he was able to present them as usual because I saw him reading the news on TV.

PART II

CHAPTER XXVIII

At last, Wednesday of the following week came when I had to meet with my editor. He was waiting for me at the Coffee Tavelli, sitting at a table next to a window. When I approached his table, he recognized me. Then when he raised his hand in greeting, he knocked over a glass of juice that he was drinking. A waitress rushed to clean the mess as I smiled and greeted the editor whose face was flushed red with embarrassment. After we introduced ourselves, I sat in front of him at the table.

"Your manuscript?" the editor asked.

"Yes," I said passing him the original of the novel.

While he was reading the manuscript, we ordered orange juice and cake.

"I like your descriptions," the editor said.

"Thanks," I smiled, looking into his eyes.

We spent a long time talking about the theme of the novel. There was a pleasant music in the background.

"Would it be OK if we have another meeting next Monday in my office?" he asked.

We agreed to get together on Monday of next week at ten a. m. As we left the cafe, he looked the original as if it was something very important.

"I'll read it carefully and I'll tell you my opinion," the editor said.

"Yes please, be honest," I said.

"Yes," he smiled. "I'm very demanding."

And he burst out laughing and I laughed nervously.

"I'm very grateful that you became interested in my novel," I said.

"I'll read the manuscript and I'll give it back to you when we meet again," he said as we parted with a kiss.

Then, he got into his vehicle and I got into mine. In my Range Rover, I drove by Providencia Avenue towards downtown of Santiago. I needed cash to buy paper and a flash drive. Therefore, I had to go to the bank to change some dollars. As I drove, I smiled happily as I thought that my novel had the potential of becoming a best-selling novel.

That day, there was not much traffic. While waiting for the light to turn green, I turned up the volume of the radio to hear a romantic song that I liked. It made me cry as I thought about the meaning of my novel. On both sides of the street, there were display cases full of clothing. People walked on the sidewalks, some wore sports clothing while others more traditional ones. Later, I passed in front of several restaurants. There was meat pie and French fries aroma coming from some restaurants. I had eaten, but I felt like parking and going inside a restaurant to eat a few meat pies. About twenty minutes later, the traffic stopped when I turned right. While waiting, I remembered that there was a protest march of students toward the center of Santiago. All vehicles began to beep their horns. On the sides of the street, people were boarding and getting off buses. After a while, I perceived a strong smell of sulfur.

Ahead, I saw on the street a group of people jostling each other. Some of them held signs with letters that read, "Better Education." Then, I felt a sensation as if I had had onion juice or sand in my eyes. The police had thrown tears gas to disperse the protesters. The students ran screaming in all directions as they rubbed their eyes desperately. I closed the windows of my Range Rover, but I still felt desperate and angry. Then, I felt nauseous. Outside, I could hear the cries of the students and police officers trying to calm the situation.

About an hour later, I could leave the protest site when I turned right again. I finally got to a bank, but it was closed. The bank's workers like students were also protesting. In front of the bank, there were many papers on the floor with various slogans. I could not enter the bank. Minutes later, I left the chaos and parked in front of another bank. There, I could change dollars and then returned to my Range Rover. After that, I left downtown Santiago as quickly as I could and later I drove by Providencia. Soon, I was going about a hundred miles an hour in the Costanera Roadway because I wanted to get home quickly. A while later, when I tried to call home, I realized that the battery of my cell phone was low.

CHAPTER XXIX

When I got home, I parked the Range Rover in the yard and then went inside. My family was having dinner. They all asked me, "How did it go?"

"It went very well. But I never expected that I was going to be stuck in traffic in the middle of a protest in downtown Santiago."

"It's horrible. They are showing the protest live on TV," one of my sisters said.

"Now, let's talk about your meeting with the editor," another sister asked.

"He accepted the manuscript and is going to read it and let me know how he finds it."

"Victoria, our father will be remembered as an inspiration by our family and others around the world," one of my brothers said.

"Yes, but these are my memories, so maybe we can write another book with all your individual recollections," I said.

"Wow, that's a wonderful idea!" I said excitedly.

That night, after supper, we sat on sofas in the living room while listening to relaxing classical music. In front, there were the big windows and a beautiful chandelier that shone from the ceiling. For a while, I leaned back on the sofa and thought about my novel. Outside the house, we could hear the barking of our dog, Max, that had been spoiled by my dad, but now, my mom spoils him.

That day, we went to bed early. I took my boots off sitting on my queen-sized bed that had a pink bedspread and white sheets. My bedroom had a large window that opened to a balcony. For a while, I sat in bed and read the novel. Before falling asleep, I looked at the light coming through the window. As I did, I remembered when my parents distributed gifts for Christmas. We were so happy that we screamed with pure joy.

The next day, I woke up before dawn. Quietly I got up, turned on the light, and then walked to the library. In the psychology section, I found a book on cognitive psychology that was high on the bookshelf. I tiptoed to grab it. With it in hand, I sat at a desk and then started leafing through it. I could not concentrate on it when I remembered my father and tears rolled down my cheeks. After a while, I stood at the window. Outside, the wind blew and shook the leaves of the trees.

CHAPTER XXX

It was still dark, so I went back to bed and dreamt that I was married to an Englishman, and we had a five-year-old daughter. She had big blue eyes. When we were boarding a plane to England, I woke up. I smiled when I remembered the dream as the sun was coming through the window.

For a while, I lay in bed remembering the images in the dream. But I felt very sad when the dream reminded me of a cognitive psychology professor who fell in love with me, but committed suicide jumping off a cliff when he thought I did not love him. Tears rolled down when I thought that the truth was that I was in love with him and I had a hard time getting over his death. Then, I went downstairs to have breakfast with the rest of my family.

After breakfast, we went to the house of my sister Magaly. That morning was very cold. We wore sweaters and pants under long coats and left for her house that was in San Bernardo. The road was clear at that time. The Range Rover was going at eighty miles per hour. After we turned into the driveway to my sister's house, we drove up the driveway and finally arrived in front of the mansion. We stopped the vehicle and a worker who was walking in the yard ran to greet us. After we met our sister with kisses and embraces, we walked inside the two-story house. Inside the living room, there were still some portraits of the family. After we sat on sofas in the living room, we talked.

Then, we stood to look around. Walking down a hallway with a high ceiling, I looked at portraits of the family on both sides. I noticed that some of the family portraits that used to be in the staircase were moved to the hallway. In front of one of them, I stood to look at the portrait of my father.

"My father looks very well and lives in our memories," I thought, looking at his portrait.

"He looks well," Magaly said.

"Yes," I said.

Afterward, when I looked at some photographs, he looked the same as I remembered him in a bathing suit at the beach. His English style distinguished himself with his family. I remembered when I saw him before I went to the United States. Then, my sister told me to follow her into the living room.

"Victoria, sit down, I want to show you something," she said.

My sister showed me pictures of my father before he died. As I looked at them, tears dropped from my eyes.

"He was always photogenic," Magaly said.

I took a photo album to look at. I was looking at it when my sister told me that they had taken them in Reñaca beach when they had gone to a country club for doctors. She and her husband were doctors. I tried very hard to hide my tears from my sister when I saw my father looking very thin in one of the pictures. Then, we looked at other photographs where my father was in the farm in the south of Chile.

"In the summer, the wheat fields were an excitement for my father," Magaly said.

"From the sky, he still has to look after his country estate," I said.

Then, my mother came into the living room and sat next to us.

"Victoria, are you looking at the photographs that we took this summer?" my mother said.

"Yes, Mommy," I replied.

"Tell me about Daddy, why did he become so thin?" I asked.

"He was well, but grew thin suddenly a few months ago," my mother said.

"I didn't know," I answered and then all of a sudden I began to cry.

That summer of 2008, was the last time he visited his large house in Yungay and his farm. But he was not feeling well. He walked slower. But his brain was impeccable.

Inside the house, there was the smell of fried onions. They were preparing lunch in the kitchen. Later, Magaly invited us to the dining room to sit at the table. Before we went there, we went to the bathrooms to wash our hands. Then, at the dinner table, I sat in front of my sister Yannette, my brothers were at the sides, and my mom at the head of the table. In the center of the table, there was red wine and a basket full of bread. My brother Hugo was responsible for uncorking the bottles of wine. After we filled the glasses, we toasted for the harmony of the family, touching our glasses. As we ate, we talked. We ate lobster with tossed salad, pea chicken soup, and grilled beef with tomato salad. For dessert, we had strawberries with chocolate syrup and chestnuts. A maid was serving us and made sure that nothing was missing at the table.

My sister liked classical music. The fireplace warmed the house. Then, the maid noticed that the glasses were empty and filled them.

"Thanks," Magaly said.

We continued eating and talking.

"I like chicken soup," I said.

"I always prepared chicken soup," my mom said.

"Yes and also beans with squash," Carmen said.

After we ate, we talked and drank. We stood from the table and sat in the living room. After a few hours, my mom said that we should return.

"What?" Magaly asked.

"We're going to go back," my mother said.

"It's still early, Mommy," Magaly said.

"Yes, but Victoria has to finish her novel," my mother said.

"Why such a hurry?" Magaly asked.

"Because of the publicity for my novel," I replied.

Sometime later, the maid offered us coffee while we talked.

"How happy we're to have you here!" Magaly said.

"So many years that you did not come," Carmen said.

"You must be visiting for a long time," Magaly said.

"Yes," I smiled.

"Victoria, how long are you going to stay here?" Magaly

asked.

"For two months," I said.

"I wish you could stay longer," my mother said.

"I'll try to return in the summer," I said.

We drank the coffee and then my sister served us cake on a tray.

"I like cake a lot," I said.

"You all like it," my mother said.

"Do you want to return to the United States?" Yannette asked.

"Yes, but I also want to be here," I replied.

That night, after we said goodbye, we walked by the side of the garden towards the Range Rover. In the vehicle, Hugo drove and our mom sat beside him. The others sat in the back. It was late. Outside it was cold. The cold breeze was coming through one of the windows. On both sides of the street, there were leafless trees. Some fallen leaves looked wet on the green grass. We passed through the center of San Bernardo. Then, we turned right. There were houses that looked alike without gardens but a lot of graffiti on the walls. The windows had iron bars protecting the houses. Occasionally, we saw a vehicle or a person walking down the street wearing a parka. The lights of the houses were almost all off.

CHAPTER XXXI

Going back, the lamps on both sides of the road lit the empty road. Occasionally, we heard the screeching brakes of other vehicles. On the way to Santiago, we remembered the past.

"This night reminds me of the times when we traveled to the south for the harvesting season," I said.

"This year we'll go to the harvesting without our dad," said Yannette, who was his youngest daughter and his spoiled child.

Through tears, I thought that hopefully things would not change much with the absence of my father. My family was rich, so I worried that some of my brothers were to ask for his or her inheritance. I knew that many wealthy families had been destroyed because of fights over that.

The Range Rover was going about a hundred miles an hour.

"Why don't you decrease the speed?" I said.

"Here we drive fast," my sister said.

Then, Yani turned the volume up on the radio when it played the song "Foreigner," in English, which was very popular when we were younger.

"This song is very beautiful," my brother Hugo said.

"Yes. In Hawaii I went to a concert of this singer," I said.

"How interesting!" my mother said.

I told them how the singer was and then we talked of other things.

Later, it began to drizzle. It was a little cold. The starry night was beautiful. It looked like those summer nights when we went to the south. The road trip lasted about an hour. Then, we entered downtown Santiago. At that time, there was a lot of noise in the city and many people were walking in all directions with colorful clothes.

As we drove, I opened my cellular and read, "I love you," a message from Pierre. He had tried to call me but I did not hear the cellular.

Minutes later, we passed the Central Station area. We saw many large houses converted into businesses, with its walls lined with graffiti on both sides of Alameda Avenue. This was different than before. That day, the road was divided into two, one for taxis and buses and the other one for private cars. I had noticed that most Chileans detested the buses because they often broke down, so many people became angry for arriving late or missing work.

Gradually, through conversations and news on TV, I noticed that many people were very dissatisfied with the Transantiago buses. I also felt sadness and compassion for people suffering because of the malfunction of those buses. Later, the rain stopped when we entered Providencia. In the windows of some shops with lights on both sides of the avenue, we saw women and men's clothing stores.

"I would like to come to buy clothes," I said as we watched the windows.

"Let's go to the Parque Arauco tomorrow," Yannette said.

"Yes, I would love to," I replied.

That night, we agreed to go there the following day.

CHAPTER XXXII

The next day, I woke up when the sun was coming into my bedroom, but it was a little cold. I got up early, but the others had already gotten up. When I walked to the balcony of the dining room, I found some of my brothers walking and looking at the birds that were chirping in the trees around the pool.

"How joyfully the thrushes chirp!" I said.

"Hello, hello, Victoria, how did you sleep?" Hugo said.

For a while we talked enthusiastically. Then, I went to have breakfast with them. That morning, the children were excited to go to play in the garden because they wanted to compete in jumping. So, they ate quickly and then ran to the garden. They got there before us. A while later, we looked at the children as they jumped singing songs in English that I had taught them. The pink-cheeked children laughed more with joyful excitement when they saw us.

Then, Ramon, one of the funniest workers, appeared in

the garden with a rabbit in his arms. The children ran to pet the rabbit.

"Do you like the bunny?" Ramon asked with a warm smile.

The children responded almost in chorus, "Yes. . ."

As I looked at the children laughing happily amidst nature, I thought about Rousseau's philosophy that says that parents should let their children explore playfully in nature. Then, we remembered how happy we were when we played hide and seek among the rosebushes.

"Yes, but do you remember that we loved to jump, too?" I said smiling.

"It fascinated me," Yannette said.

Then, the worker left the children with the rabbit and began to prune the rose bushes around the garden.

"These roses grow much better when we prune them," the gardener said.

"Yes," we said.

Then, we left the worker and walked to the pool with the kids. As we walked we talked.

Yannette said, "My father loved his fruit trees that he had planted."

"Now, he must be looking from the sky how his workers take good care of them," I said.

"My father with compassion covered the cracks on the trees because he loved agriculture," Yannette said.

"Yes, he loved his trees like humans. Sometimes, when they swayed, he watered them to grow and to give good fruits," I said.

"He loved nature very much, so he sometimes pruned the grape vines for the vines not to grow better."

"It was as if the tree had been human," Yannette said.

My father liked to share the love of nature with his children. In that way, we remembered the past.

"The legacy that our father left us was the love for nature," continued Yannette.

"Yes," I replied.

At lunch, we returned to the house. Then, we went to the shopping mall Parque Arauco.

In the shopping mall, we walked through the middle of a marble hallway. There were many shops with large windows showing the clothes of the season. I looked at the windows happily. Sometimes, we stopped in front of some shops and entered.

"I like those white boots," I said looking at a display case.

"Oh, they're very nice," my mother said.

We entered the shoe store, I sat on a sofa, and a saleswoman brought me some boots and I tried them on. They fit me very well. They were made of leather.

"They're the best boots. It's the best leather," the saleswoman said.

"They're pretty and they look good on you," Yannette said.

"Well, I'll buy them, but please bring me more boots of the same quality, but in other colors," I said.

"Yes, of course," the saleswoman said.

As I tried the boots, I smiled thinking about how Pierre would find them. I bought several pairs, in white, brown, and beige. I had an obsession for high-heeled long boots and I loved to put my pants inside them like for polo sport.

"Is there anything else you want to see miss?" The saleswoman asked.

"Yes, I want to buy a white leather belt," I said while my mom and Yannette tried some boots and shoes enthusiastically. They also had an obsession for shoes.

We bought several things and then left the shoe store and went to buy more clothes. Because of so much walking, our feet hurt. Then, when we saw a restaurant, we went in because we were thirsty and hungry. After we sat at a table, we ordered steak with tossed greens and French fries. We drank orange juice.

My mother said, "I enjoyed shopping."

"This mall had a good selection of clothing," I said.

"Yes, but is it as good as in Hawaii?"

"Yes, this shopping mall is like any other mall in New York or Europe."

After we ate, we continued window-shopping for leather jackets. But they did not have the ones I wanted, so I had to order one, which would come the next week. Then we returned home.

CHAPTER XXXIII

Next week on Friday, I went back to the Parque Arauco to get the leather jacket that I ordered, but this time I went alone. That day, the shopping mall was very crowded. When I got to the store, I asked the saleswoman if my jacket had arrived.

"Yes, ma'am. Do you want to try it on?" the saleswoman asked.

"Yes, of course!" I said.

I tried it on and it was fine. I bought it and left the store smiling as I thought about how Pierre would find my jacket.

Outside, as I walked and looked at the windows wondering about what else I could buy, all of a sudden, Pierre was right in front of me. He looked very elegant with his shorter hair and Polo sportswear. We greeted with a kiss and hug. I was wearing a white sweater, light brown pants, white boots, and a light brown jacket. We felt happy to have met by surprise. I found him more attractive.

Leaving the shopping mall, I realized I had spent a lot of time in the mall. We continued walking and passed in front of many restaurants. Ahead, we stopped at one that had tables with umbrellas. We sat at one of them that reminded me of the ones I had seen in Paris where the writer Hemingway had sat and described in his novels. All around us, some people ate French fries and drank Coca-Cola or milkshakes while talking on their cell phones.

We took the menu that was on the table and we both ordered strawberry milkshake. That day the restaurant was not so crowded. While we drank the milkshake, we talked.

"Why didn't you tell me that you were going shopping?" Pierre asked.

"Oh, darling. Next time."

"Can I see what you bought?"

"Yes, why not?" I replied smiling.

As I took out my jacket from the bag and showed it to him, he said,

"It looks beautiful."

We continued talking and he told me that he liked to go to that shopping mall because they had very good clothes. When we finished the milkshakes, he told me that he had to go to his office and asked me to accompany him. His office at the TV station was nearby. As we walked, it began to drizzle. The leaves of the trees were swaying and dripping water. Soon, it was raining in torrents. Pierre opened his umbrella and told me to take his arm. We walked fast to avoid getting wet. Although it was a sudden rain, Pierre had his umbrella.

When we had walked about a block, a gust of wind turned the umbrella inside out and it flipped away from Pierre's hands. Pierre ran after it laughing as I watched him. The water was running down our faces and soaking our clothes. Pierre got the umbrella. We walked quickly to the parking lot. As we walked, Pierre whispered,

"I love you, Victoria!"

At that moment, I saw some delicious cakes and pies in the window of a bakery. They made me hungry.

"How about if we go in to eat cake?" Pierre said.

"I'd love to, but I'm on a diet," I smiled.

"Eat one. I don't think it is going to make you fat," Pierre said.

"All right."

In the bakery, we smiled while we chose a cake. After we sat at a table, we ordered one with nuts. As I ate, I thought I liked Pierre, but I would miss him when going back to the States.

"Are you worried?" he said.

"No, why?" I asked.

"You look worried."

After we ate, we left. Outside, it was still raining. We ran through the rain to the parking lot. In his vehicle, we went to his office. On the way back, Pierre invited me to his house, but I told him that I would like to, but I had to revise the chapters I had written in the morning.

"Oh, honey, let's go to my home," he said.

"Another day, honey."

"Okay my love, but tell me that you love me," Pierre said.

"I love you, I love you," I said lovingly while Pierre interrupted me with a kiss that left me breathless.

Then, he drove me home. Along the way, he squeezed my hand in his.

Back home. I went to my bedroom and lay in bed thinking

of Pierre. He did the same when he got back to his home. I saw him several times that week and we agreed to play tennis on Saturday the next weekend.

CHAPTER XXXIV

Pierre and I met almost every day. The next weekend on Saturday, the sun was shining and it was a little cold when Pierre arrived to the mansion of my family. He smiled with delight when I appeared on the balcony upstairs.

"Bonjour, Victoria! How are you?" he waved at me.

"Bonjour. Ready to play tennis," I said smiling.

Then, I went down to the terrace where I greeted Pierre with a kiss. Some of my brothers and sisters also waited to play tennis with us.

"Since it's cold, it's very good to play tennis!" Pierre said.

"Yes, very good," I said.

Then, I went to get my racket. The others had theirs in their hands. Soon, we left for the tennis courts talking with excitement. Pierre placed his hands on my shoulders and turned me toward him and kissed me. I was wearing sports clothing that I had bought in Paris when I was a doctorate student in French literature at the Sorbonne University.

"You look very pretty," Pierre whispered in my ear.

I smiled and said, "Thank you . . . it's a reminder of the Sorbonne."

Then, as we walked to the tennis court, I thought of my father who sometimes played tennis. Then, while we played tennis, some leaves fell on the tennis court.

My mom was talking to some friends of the mother's club. They often met to talk about activities to benefit the poor.

While playing tennis with Pierre, I thought I liked him and I found him very handsome.

That day, Pierre and I wore light blue and white sportswear by coincidence and looked like a couple. After a while, we competed while some of my brothers and sisters clapped sitting on a green bench on one side of the tennis court.

"Victoria is winning," one of them shouted happily, while the others screamed and clapped filled with excitement.

"Wait a little longer and I'll also win!" Pierre said graciously.

Then another person won and at the end we all won at least one match.

After we played tennis, Pierre and I sat in the garden beside the pool while the others walked inside the house.

"Look, Pierre!" I said pointing to the water in the pool.

"What?" Pierre asked curiously.

"The view looks like a scene from a painting by Monet," I replied.

"Oh, yes, you're right," Pierre said.

"Do you think Monet resembles Hemingway?" I said.

"Of course, because like Hemingway, Monet also shows descriptions of the different seasons of the year," Pierre said.

The sun shone and a refreshing breeze rose.

Birds chirped around us like in the spring.

"What's the most important thing for a writer?" Pierre asked me.

"A passion for writing," I said.

"I think that writing is a mystery to be discovered by writing," Pierre said.

"Yes, it's true. The writer creates a world with words," I said.

Through the window, I saw my brother Hugo who was reading a newspaper while drinking juice. My mom walked from one room to another. That afternoon, Pierre invited me out to dinner and we were to get together at seven.

CHAPTER XXXV

At the appointed time, Pierre picked me up. I was not ready yet. He waited sitting on a couch in the living room listening to music. A maid served him a raspberry juice as he waited for me. Pierre could not wait to see me, so he looked at his watch nervously. When I was ready, I went downstairs anticipating having fun with Pierre. He smiled happily when he greeted me with a kiss. Then, we left. That day, he wore a dark suit, white shirt, a maroon tie, and light brown shoes. While the vehicle moved amid the heavy traffic, sometimes, Pierre took my hand in his and said, "*Je t'aime.*"

"*Moi, aussi.*"

"When I don't see you, I miss you very much," Pierre told me lovingly as he kissed me.

It was warm inside the vehicle, but it was very cold outside. On the radio, they said it was only ten degrees Celsius. As we passed in front of Almacenes Paris shopping mall, I remembered my father when we went there to buy gifts for Christmas.

In autumn, it got dark earlier and it was very cold. The streetlights illuminated a little. When we reached the restaurant, Pierre got out first and opened the car door for me. Then, we walked toward the restaurant. Pierre had reserved a table next to a window.

After we sat at the table, a waiter came to take our order. With the menu in hand, we ordered dinner.

"Roast lamb with mashed potatoes and tomato salad. For dessert, peaches with cream," I said.

"Thank you, how about you, sir?" the waiter asked Pierre.

"The same, please, but add lettuce salad and a bottle of red wine."

We talked as we waited for the food and wine. There was classical music in the background. That day there were many people.

Soon, the waiter returned with the food trays. In the middle of the table, he put the bottle of red wine and the food in front of each of us. Before we started to eat, we toasted with red wine for our love.

"The wine is very sweet," Pierre said savoring it.

"Yes, very good," I said.

Then, we began to eat while we talked. I noticed that he had combed his hair differently.

"Why did you comb your hair differently?" I asked Pierre.

He smiled and said, "Do you really want to know?"

"Yes."

Pierre told me that when he went to study journalism at Harvard University in Boston, Massachusetts, he had worked for the CIA in the United States. So, sometimes, he was afraid to live in Chile because he could have been mistaken for a spy. At that time, there were many Chilean secret agents who tracked Chileans with foreign ties.

In front of the restaurant in Vitacura, there was a luxurious hotel from which he saw a secret agent who worked for the United Nations coming out. He had met him in the United States.

He said that at that time it was dangerous to have been an ex-member of the CIA

"Why?" I asked.

"Because we were paid to eat at fancy restaurants to get information from criminals, corrupt people, or to teach others how to behave as secret agents," Pierre said.

We continued eating and talking. From time to time, the waiter came to see us if we needed anything. Inside, it was quite warm. I was always interested in everything that had to do with secret agents and especially the North American and British ones, so I listened excitedly and with curiosity. Then we talked of other things.

"How are you doing with your novel?" Pierre asked.

"Every day I like what I write," I said smiling.

"How will it end?" Pierre asked with curiosity.

"With its publication," I replied, smiling, as I wasn't sure about it yet.

Then, a group of women came in and I became jealous when Pierre looked at one of them who was looking at him from a table across the restaurant.

"Do you know her?" I asked.

"Why do you ask?" Pierre asked.

"You looked at her!" I said.

"Love, don't be jealous," Pierre said nervously.

"Me, jealous?" I said a little upset.

"Yes, my love."

"I'm not jealous," I said suggesting going home.

Pierre shrugged his shoulders as he apologized for having looked at that woman. I pretended that I was not jealous, but I was extremely angry because I had felt humiliated when he looked at the other woman.

A while later, we stood and left the restaurant. As we walked out, he said,

"When can we meet again?"

"I don't know," I replied angrily.

"Why?"

"I think we should not see each other again," I said.

"Don't tell me that," Pierre protested.

"I think it's better," I said.

"Victoria, please listen to me," Pierre said.

For a while, we walked in silence. Later, he tried to kiss me but I did not let him because I was still angry. He tried again and I still did not let him by turning my face. I walked faster. About a block ahead, it began to drizzle while Pierre was approaching me.

"Victoria, please listen to me," he said.

Before arriving at the next block, Pierre reached me, took my arm, and kissed me, but I slapped him and continued walking. Nervous and desperate, he stood at the edge of the sidewalk and saw me leave his side hurriedly without turning my head back. As I walked away from him, I felt I loved him, but my pride wanted to humiliate him and that he should beg me for forgiveness. Before I disappeared, Pierre ran behind me soaked by the rain saying, "I love you, I love you."

I kept walking because I wanted him to feel bad for having humiliated me. Sometimes, I swallowed some water running down my face. Further ahead, he took my arm and told me.

"I know that you love me."

"No," I replied.

"You're lying," Pierre said distressed.

"You're wrong," I said.

Then when we walked beside a tree, he took my arm again.

"Tell me that you don't love me," Pierre said.

"I don't love you," I said.

"I love you," he told me and hugged me and kissed me hard in his arms.

We were all alone in the rain, darkness, and cold. As he tightened in his arms around me, I felt his heartbeat. I was a little frigid sexually, but at that moment I desired him and I felt more and more excited. The more he kissed me, the more I could not resist him. I really wanted him to make love to me. "I love you," he kept whispering in my ear panting as he yearned for me and kept on filling me with pleasure. It was cold and windy. Sometimes, I giggled when he bit by lips. There I was with Pierre filled with desire. I came from a culture in which it was forbidden to speak about sensual longing, but I felt very North American and free to let Pierre love me. When we heard a sound, we stopped and walked away filled with lust and desire. The wind shook the branches of the trees and dropped raindrops on us.

"It's freezing!" I said.

"We're almost in the parking lot."

I let him kiss me while the raindrops from the trees fell on our faces. Then, we walked to the parking lot.

"Did you like it?" he asked.

"It was a little sadistic."

"Why?"

"Because I slapped you then you kissed me and bit my lips."

"Instinctively. After the reconciliation, I felt stronger for you."

As we walked, I thought that he was right that love was better after the reconciliation. We crossed a main avenue, and we arrived to the parking lot. Pierre wanted to meet the next day, but I told him that I had to think about it and that I would call him.

On the way home, I thought that if someone was looking at us from inside a fence of a garden, he or she might have felt excited by looking at us shivering with desire and pleasure. The car lights beamed on the wet ground.

When I got to my parent's home, Pierre kissed me and then I got out of the vehicle and ran inside the house not to get wet. Some family members had gone to sleep, others were watching television, and the rest were chatting in the living room.

That night, I went to the library to correct any errors in my novel. Some of my brothers were reading there. While reviewing a chapter of my novel, my brother came to talk to me.

"What do you think about Pierre?" He asked.

"Well. I like him. He is very handsome."

"He is known as a Don Juan."

"How do you know?" I asked.

"The other day I saw him walking with a woman and then I saw him with another."

Hearing that, I hid my indignation and anger when I said," But if they were not holding hands, maybe they could have been friends."

"They were holding hands," Hugo said.

"Hand in hand?" I asked skeptically.

"No, I was just kidding," Hugo said laughing.

"What a disgusting joke!" I said.

My sister, Yannette, who noticed that I felt angry, told my brother smiling from the couch where she was reading, "Could it be that you say that because you're a Don Juan?"

"Me, a Don Juan?" Hugo asked.

"Yes," Yannette said.

"No," Hugo said trying to put an end to the conversation.

My brother was very jealous of us, so it was hard for him to accept our suitors.

Then, I went to bed. In my bedroom, on the second floor, there was still the same bed that I had when I was a teenager. I lit the lamp that was on the nightstand and opened the window that opened to a balcony. The bed was next to the big window. In the summer, I saw my younger brothers when they climbed the cherry, plum, or apple trees.

Before I went to bed that night, we sat on the bed and talked about my novel.

"I know that you will have great success with it," one of my sisters said.

I smiled with the originals in my hand and said, "I hope so."

As we talked, I listened to some of my brothers who were chatting in the living room. Others had already gone to bed.

Then, my mom came to see me in my bedroom. She brought us fresh cow's milk. She also sat on the bed.

My mom took the novel in her hands and said, "Victoria, you write very well!"

"Thank you, Mom," I said.

That night, we spoke until the wee hours and almost did not sleep at all talking.

That night, through the balcony of my bedroom, I looked at the shining stars as I thought about Pierre. I missed him and had a hard time putting him out of my mind. In his house, Pierre turned side to side as he imagined how he would kiss me next to him. He smiled as he remembered when he pulled me against a tree and if it was not for the sound we heard who knows what we could have done. Then, he wondered that someone could have been peering at us, but then he reasoned that there was nobody but us.

CHAPTER XXXVI

I waited a week to meet the editor again. That Monday, I got up at sunrise because I had an appointment with him at ten o'clock. The hours passed quickly as I sat behind my desk to write a summary of the novel. I sensed that the novel would be a success. The sun was coming through the window. The hills were covered with grass and the peaks with snow.

In the backyard, I heard the workers who were beginning to sweep the leaves. At that time, many leaves fell from the trees. For a while, I stood behind the window and thought about my father who liked to get up early at the time of wheat harvesting in the summer. But now, my father existed only in memory.

Optimistically, I showered, changed clothes, had breakfast, and left for the office of the publisher. Many people walked on both sides of the street. The sky was blue, but it was cold. The birds were chirping everywhere.

I had driven about five minutes when a romantic song

by Cold Play began to play on the radio. I turned the volume up and smiled. Some people looked at me and smiled. I was happy.

Then, I accelerated my Range Rover to arrive there faster. Within minutes, I arrived at the office of the publisher. I parked the Range Rover in front and then walked toward the entrance. I climbed the stairs and rang the bell.

"Yes, I'm coming," the editor said walking to open the door. "Hello! I was waiting for you, how are you?"

"Well, thank you and you," I replied.

He invited me to sit in front of his desk.

"Your novel is very well written," he said, lifting the original with his right hand.

"Thanks," I said smiling.

"You just have to correct some details and it will be ready for publication. If you have time, we can revise it now," the editor said.

"Yes, of course, let's do it," I replied.

Then, one of his secretaries offered me coffee. I accepted it, and we continued reviewing the manuscript of the novel until we made all the corrections.

"I also brought the summary," I said.

"Good!" He said as he received it.

As he read it, he said it was excellent. Then, he looked at me and spoke about the publishing contract. I accepted it.

"Oh, thank God," I laughed with joy.

"Yes, Victoria, many bookstores have already requested your book."

It seemed like a dream that my novel was a success.

"Thank God," I said to the editor again when I said goodbye with a kiss.

I left his office happily. As I walked to the Range Rover, people smiled at me. In my vehicle, I put a CD with a song that added to my happiness. I still could not believe it. The editor told me that in about twenty days, there would be printed the first copies of my novel. During the wait, my anxiety grew day by day and I just wanted the time to pass quickly. The days seemed longer. Time seemed to stand still, until finally the expected day came. That morning when I got the call from the editor in which he said that the book was ready, I dressed quickly and rushed to the editor's office. I arrived there very quickly. When I had the book in my hands, my excitement made me laugh like a little girl. My happiness was complete. I was living a dream come true. The editor took me out of that state asking me,

"Would you like to sign autographs in two weeks?"

"Of course, but wouldn't it be too soon," I replied happily.

"It's all right."

"Then, I accept it."

He said that it would be in the bookstore, "The Book." When we finished talking, I got into my vehicle and I accelerated it. I took about fifteen minutes to get home. There, I went straight to find my mom to show her my book that had just been printed. Then, my whole family came to know my book. It was like having a newborn son. Everyone was excited. It seemed that the book was theirs. Then, Pierre came and hugged me with a kiss to congratulate me for my novel. I was surprised that Pierre was there waiting for me.

That night as we ate in the dining room on the second floor, the only thing that we talked about was my book.

Later, we went to the living room. There, my family and Pierre continued talking about my novel. For a while, I stood with Pierre behind the living room window watching the starry sky that reminded me of summer nights we spent in the wheat field.

"My love, do you see a bright golden star in the sky that stands out among the rest?" I asked Pierre.

"Yes, it has to be the morning star."

Looking at it, Pierre kissed me and whispered, "It's a distinctive star like you my love."

"Then, we'll call it, the star of our love, and when I go back to the United States it will remind me of our love when I see it."

"Yes, my love, but I don't want you to go back."

Embraced, we contemplated the star that united us anywhere in the world.

That night, I spoke with my family and Pierre all about my novel. They congratulated me again and again.

Pierre had to do a news report the following morning, so he went home that night.

CHAPTER XXXVII

That night, I went to sleep very late. I put on my pajamas in my bedroom, moved the curtains, and looked out through the balcony. As I looked out, I thought happily about my novel which was ready and that I was falling in love with Pierre. Outside, it was foggy. The lamps in the backyard lit the leaves on the trees. The autumn breeze was cold. For a while, I looked at the foliage. Then, I went to bed and fell asleep. I dreamed I was at a gala party in World War II. In the dream, I saw a large mansion that had high pillars. At the entrance, there was a garden with many trees. Inside, there were people dressed in fine clothing, who talked cheerfully. Others were sitting at a long dining room table. The buzz of conversations was heard amidst the music that was like a bolero. The house had hallways with high ceilings that led to dining rooms. There were chandeliers in all the rooms. Some people danced.

Then, I turned to the right and the dream changed a bit.

I was walking with my family among other families to a port. There, my brothers, my sisters, and I were young children. We played and shouted on the pier while my mom and dad were watching us. Other families did the same. In the dream, my father was going to sail as an officer in honor of Prime Minister Churchill in the British navy during the Second World War. As we played, we heard the ship's loudspeaker asking the officers to go in the ship. My father with a hug and kiss said good-bye to each of his children and my mom. Then, he walked to the ship and boarded it. From the deck, he waved goodbye to us while the ship moved slowly away towards the horizon. We cried, as we tried to see him, but the ship finally disappeared in the mist.

On the way home, the breeze and the rain wet our faces. Later, I felt sad when I heard the sound of an airplane. I woke before dawn. When I looked through the balcony, it was drizzling outside. For a while, I remembered the dream, which made me feel sad when I thought about its content. Then, I went to bed again and fell asleep.

When I awoke in the morning, the warm sun was coming inside my bedroom. I got up and opened the window that opened into a balcony and felt the cool breeze as I thought about Pierre. I thought that I was going to tell him about another book I had written about learning.

PART III

✹

CHAPTER XXXVIII

A **week after** I told Pierre that I had written a book about learning, he wanted Edward Brighton, one of his best friends who was a reporter on TV, Channel 5, to interview me about the book. I told him that I was very busy in the advertising of the novel about my father, but he convinced me that we meet with Edward. We agreed to meet with Edward in a restaurant at eight in the evening on the weekend.

At seven o'clock on Friday evening, Pierre picked me up to introduce me to his friend. I was getting dressed. After Pierre waited for me talking to my brother Hugo, I grabbed a copy of my book and we left. Days before I had given a copy to Pierre and he had read it. On the way there, we talked.

"Do you like my book?" I asked.

"Very much," he answered. "May I ask you why you wrote it?"

"For my dissertation in Cognitive Psychology."

"How interesting!"

As we talked, I thought about the experiment on cognitive psychology I had conducted years ago. I saw the scene of the experiment: a large computer that controlled the computers of the students who voluntarily participated.

Then, the radio began to play a song I liked. I turned the volume up and looked ahead while listening to the song. Then, we continued talking.

"What did you like the most about my book?" I asked.

"The quick way to learn that you teach," he answered.

The vehicle's heating made me perspire. I opened the window. Outside, the breeze moved the branches of the trees. When we were near the restaurant, Pierre looked at me passionately as we talked. I noticed that he liked me very much.

"Learning is a very controversial issue," Pierre said.

"Yes, there are many students who think that memorizing is learning. But, learning is understanding," I replied.

"Yes, that's true," he said.

Then, we arrived at the restaurant and parked in front of the entrance. We got out of the Range Rover. Upon entering, I saw a tall, blond man with large deep blue eyes who distinguished himself from afar, but he had an air of arrogance. He was Edward, who had already arrived. He was sitting at a table beside a large window overlooking a swimming pool. Pierre introduced me to Edward who greeted me with a kiss. Edward seemed younger and thinner than Pierre. Both Edward and Pierre looked stunning in dark suits, ties, and light shirts. Edward found me very young and sexy. I took a copy of my book from my bag and put it on the table in front of him. Pierre and I sat down. I noticed that Edward had a copy of my book with notes that were apparent at the edges.

"I was anxious to meet you," Edward said to me.

I smiled and said, "Here, I am."

"Is she more beautiful and charming than you thought?" Pierre said lovingly.

"Yes, much more beautiful and elegant. On the cover of the book she appears with glasses."

I smiled.

Then, we asked for something to eat and red wine.

"Your book, *Rapid Cognition and Learning*, is very interesting," Edward said.

"Thank you," I said.

"Did you know that your book is very popular with students?" Edward asked.

"Yes, and I'm very happy about that," I answered.

Then a waiter brought us the food and wine. We ate roast beef with mashed potatoes and tomato salad.

"The food is very good," Edward said.

"Yes, very tasty," Pierre said.

Then we talked about Hawaii and Edward said that he had been in Hawaii for a conference as a foreign correspondent.

"Wow! Did you like it?" I asked.

"Oh, Honolulu is paradise." Edward said.

'You're right. The weather is always like spring and summer," I said.

"Unlike Chile that is very cold in winter and very hot and dry in the summer," Pierre said.

"Honolulu reminds me of Easter Island," Edward said.

I smiled and said, "Yes, but Honolulu is very modern because it has top universities and is well connected with the entire world."

Then, Edward asked me if he could interview me on his TV show about my book. I told him I was busy in the publicity of a novel I had written in honor of my father, but it would be fine. Although I found him a little bit arrogant, I thought he could help me to publicize my novel on television because sometimes he spoke about cultural things.

"Is it okay if I interviewed you next Monday morning?"

"Yes, what time?"

"At ten o'clock."

"Yes, all right."

We agreed to get together on the agreed date. When we finished eating, we talked a little about different things. Then, we left the restaurant. In the parking lot, Edward went to his car and Pierre and I went to the Range Rover. As Edward drove, he thought that I was fascinating; while Pierre kissed me and told me that he wanted the best for me because he loved me very much.

Sometime later, he placed his hand on mine and told me, "Let's go to my house?"

"I would like to, but I have to prepare a presentation that I have to send to the United States," I replied.

That day, he gave me a ride to my family's house.

During that week, Pierre and I met several times.

CHAPTER XXXIX

On the agreed day, at ten in the morning, I drove to the television station Channel 5 where Edward worked. I parked the vehicle in the parking lot and then walked to the front entrance door. When I arrived there, a person guided me to a studio and Edward greeted me with a kiss and invited me to sit on a brown leather chair and he sat on another chair in from of me across a glass top table in the center of the room. The TV station cameramen turned their cameras on us. Edward was dressed in an elegant blue suit, white shirt, a maroon tie, and shoes that matched his clothing. That day I was wearing a Christian Dior dress, a long coat, and high-heeled shoes. His voice sounded very confident.

At the beginning of the interview, Edward introduced me to the viewers. Then, he started asking me questions.

"What is the title of your book?"

"*Cognition and Learning Fast*," I replied.

"Please tell us, why you wrote this book?"

"Well, because I'm passionate about everything that has to do with learning," I said smiling.

"How interesting! Did you know that your book has taught many people how to learn?"

"Yes, I knew it and I am very excited that many people apply this method of learning that I teach," I said enthusiastically.

"One of the most important points that you raise is that whatever one wants to learn has to be associated with what the person already knows, has to be organized, and has to be studied spacingly," Edward said.

"Yes, that is right."

"What do you mean when you say that spaced study or study in short intervals is better than massed study?"

"I mean that it is much better to study in short intervals than spending too much time on one stretch of study"

"You're right because studying for long hours without a break is boring."

"Exactly. Spaced study has profound effects on learning."

"Could you tell me how can one elaborate the information that one wants to learn?" Edward asked.

"The information is elaborated by associating it with what is already known regarding what you want to learn, in that way the information is distinguished, learned, and encoded in long term memory. For example, when one is in love, one elaborates a boyfriend or girlfriend with thoughts, images, and fantasies that create strong memory traces. Another example would be, for instance, when you want to learn the meaning of the word Christmas, you could think about what the word means and relate it to your own experience," I said.

"So, elaborating the information that one wants to learn results in better memory," Edward said.

"Yes, that's right!" I said.

"So, when people elaborate the information they want to learn, they use their own experience to do it and that facilitates understanding and learning," Edward said excitedly.

"Yes, absolutely," I said. "Often students don't learn because the activities in the classrooms are boring and passive and don't stimulate the elaboration of the information they try to learn."

"Right, there are many students who do their best to learn, but don't know how."

Sometimes, Edward and I drank water while we talked. The air was warm.

"That means that the "how" people study is more important than the time they spend studying," Edward said.

"Yes, the quality of study is more important than the quantity or the amount of time people study," I said.

"You're absolutely right because if people just memorize whatever they're trying to learn, they might spend weeks trying to learn without learning anything. However, if they associate the information they're trying to learn with what they already know, they can learn faster," Edward said.

Edward, at times, flipped through the book in his hand as he asked me questions.

"What would you say in general about rapid learning?" Edward asked.

"Learning is faster if people elaborate, contrast, compare, organize, and study at intervals rather than repeat or memorize the information they're trying to learn."

"In your book, you also say that depression affects learning. Can you tell us how depression affects learning?"

"Many people affected by depression have a hard time

learning because they have difficulties concentrating, lack energy, and have trouble sleeping, so they might feel sleepy and have difficulties maintaining attention throughout the day. Therefore, depressed people lack enthusiasm to learn as their minds are obsessed with negative thoughts," I said.

"That means that many depressed students might feel sleepy in the classroom and not pay attention to what the teacher is saying," Edward said. "What do you recommend to reduce and prevent depression?"

"I suggest changing negative automatic thoughts for positive thoughts," I said.

"Do you mean to restructure the bad habit of negative thinking with positive thinking?" Edward asked.

"Yes . . . because many times, depression is the effect of the bad habit of negative thinking which can be changed by positive thinking," I replied.

"It's interesting how positive thoughts have powerful effects on our emotional well-being," Edward said.

"Right, because positive thoughts keep a person optimistic but pessimistic thoughts depress a person," I said.

"Your book teaches that we should fill our minds with optimistic thoughts because they enhance learning."

"That's right," I said.

"How about automatic worry thoughts?" he asked.

"You push them out of your mind and think about pleasant things," I said.

"You're right because positive thinking makes people feel good."

Edward looked at me with curiosity and excitement while he was interviewing me. I noticed that he had read the book carefully because sometimes when he opened it I saw his notes in the margin. I felt happy that he had been so interested in my book.

"You also suggest changing sedentary behavior because it might inhibit learning," Edward said.

"Yes, because many experimental psychological studies have shown that inactivity causes depression," I said.

When it came time for commercials, Edward and I stood and looked out the window. He opened it a little, looked at me, and said, "You're very beautiful!"

I smiled without knowing that Edward felt I was the woman for him.

Before continuing the interview, a person from the television station retouched my makeup. Then, Edward continued asking me questions.

"You suggest that parents can stimulate their children cognitively in simple ways. Can you tell us how?" Edward asked.

"Parents do not need to have a fortune to stimulate their children cognitively because they can just use everyday objects at home for quantitative comparisons, for example, they can tell their children to sort fruits by size, shapes, sameness, and differences in a fruit bowl. Parents then can ask them if there are more apples than oranges when they have oranges and apples in a bowl. Children have fun and make it a game and challenge each other sorting fruits. Parents can also stimulate their children when they sit at the table to have meals because, for example, they can ask their children how many plates they need to serve or which food they like the most and why?"

"That's very interesting, and the children can eat some of the fruits while they are learning. Also, in that way, they can learn subtraction automatically," Edward said, laughingly.

"Yes, it prepares them for learning subtraction later," I said smiling.

"What would you say about developmental toys," he asked.

"They are good, but children can benefit a lot by stimulating conversations with parents and friends because that enhances their cognitive development," I said

"What do you mean by cognitive development?" Edward asked me.

"The development of thoughts, memory, language, problem solving, reasoning, and imagination of children, etc." I replied.

"What would you say in general about children's cognitive stimulation?" Edward asked me.

"It's very important because many cognitive experimental studies have found that the brains of children growing up in an environment with a lot of cognitive stimulation grow and develop more neurons or brain cells than children who are not cognitively stimulated," I said.

"I strongly agree with that," Edward said.

"Yes . . . because that prepares them to reason and adjust to school better," I said.

"Is there much difference between the children entering kindergarten?"

"Of course because the children who have been stimulated cognitively get better grades, express their ideas more clearly, and share and get along with other students better than those who have not been cognitively stimulated."

"You also suggest that children before kindergarten need to know the alphabet and know how to put the letters together."

"Yes," I said.

"How interesting that you say that in the United States parents encourage their children to learn to read before entering kindergarten," the journalist said.

While he was interviewing me, I listened to the murmurs of the cameramen who focused on us. On the right side of the study, there was a television screen showing the live interview.

"Your book is very deep," Edward said.

"Yes. I wanted to include in it, the most important factors for rapid learning."

"You also say that good nutrition enhances learning. Can you tell us how?" he asked.

"Of course. Because some food makes us feel full with energy such as milk, fruits, vegetables, but junk food make us feel tired. The cells or neurons that store or recall information are formed of proteins found in milk and are the basic structures of human beings."

"Is that why you recommend a balanced diet of protein, fruits, vegetables and cereals, etc.?"

"Yes, and avoid fast or junk food because they contain substances that inhibit and interfere with learning."

"Are you against McDonald's restaurants?"

"No . . . but people should avoid fast food," I smiled.

Suddenly, I began to perceive a smell of fried onions. I looked right and I saw that next to a camera, a cameraman who was sitting on the floor was eating a meat pie without us noticing it. The cameraman smiled and stopped chewing when I looked at him. It was time for lunch.

"Let's pause and then return," Edward said before going

to another commercial.

Back to the interview, Edward removed his coat.

"Could you tell us how sports affect learning?" Edward asked me.

"Exercise reduces depression and inspires the mind and produces feelings of excitement by the dopamine secreted by the body, which enhances enthusiasm for learning," I replied.

At the end of the interview, Edward and I spoke for a while and he invited me to have lunch with him. I told him that I was very busy but maybe some other time. When I stood to leave, he thanked me and I left the TV station. As I walked to my Range Rover, I smiled happily. I thought about the interview and Edward who could interview me to publicize my novel.

That day, I had lunch with Pierre. He was very excited that I had spoken about my book on TV. After lunch, Pierre went back to work and I went back home.

In the evening, while I was having dinner with my family, we saw the interview on TV. As we ate we talked about it. They all liked it.

"You looked very well in the interview, Victoria," Yannette said.

I smiled and said, "Thanks."

One of my brothers smiled when he thought that Edward looked like a robot when he read the news.

They asked me if Edward would publicize my novel. I told them I did not know yet, but I would like that.

The next evening I went to see a movie with Pierre, but then I did not see him for some days when he went to the south of Chile to cover some news. During those days, Pierre called me every day to tell me that he loved me and missed me. I also missed him and kept busy planning the promotion and marketing of my novel. Then, when he came back, Pierre and I met almost every day.

CHAPTER XL

"Hi Victoria, I'm Edward," he told me when he called me a few days later to invite me to have dinner with him.

"I'd like to, but I'm busy," I said.

His invitation did not surprise me because I had noticed that during the interview, he looked at me insistently. I was dating Pierre. To accept his invitation would generate conflict between them. They were very good friends. I just wanted him to help me with the publicity of my novel. At first glance, I found him arrogant and domineering.

Days later, he called me again and again to invite me out, but I told him that I was busy. During those days that I rejected his invitations, he felt despair thinking that he would do anything to go out with me. Sometimes, he smiled as he lay in his bed imagining how he would love me. He exercised a lot for me to find him more attractive and desirable. For days, he daydreamed about me thinking deep down that one-day or another I would accept his invitation.

The more that I avoided going out with him; the more he wanted to go out with me. But one day, I accepted to have dinner with him even though I feared that Pierre could find out about me going out with his best friend. That day, we went to a revolving restaurant that was on top of a building in Providencia. He parked his vehicle near the restaurant. Then, we walked towards the entrance of the building. As we waited for the elevator, we looked and smiled at each other. Then, as we spoke, I noticed that he was a very good listener. Then, the elevator rose slowly, shaking on some floors. When it reached the top of the building, the door opened and we got out. We walked down a hallway to the restaurant and entered. A waiter led us to a table by the window, took the order, and then brought us a bottle of champagne. We laughed when the cork popped out when the waiter opened it. That day there were not so many people. Edward filled a glass for each of us. We raised our glasses and touched them.

"Mmm . . . it's refreshing," Edward said as he sipped his drink raising his eyebrows with pleasure.

"Yes," I smiled too.

That night, we ate roast beef with mashed potatoes and a side of tomato salad, drank red wine, and had cherries with chocolate for dessert.

"It tastes very good!" I said.

"Oh, I love it," he said.

The table was candle lit and had a white tablecloth and napkins. We could see the lights across the city and the sparkling stars in the sky. As we ate, he looked at me with a seductive smile.

"You look very beautiful in that dress," he said.

I smiled a little confused because I was romantically involved with Pierre. Edward had an air of style and elegance that I found fascinating.

He told me that he enjoyed playing tennis and had a tennis court at his house. After I told him that I also liked to play tennis, he said, "Are you this lovely on the tennis court?"

I grinned again as I found him so charming and interested in me. Then, he asked me if I was enjoying dinner.

"Yes."

"Why don't we play tennis this weekend?" he asked me.

"Let me think about it."

After dinner, we went down the elevator to the parking lot. On the way back home, we talked with excitement.

"You have a very sexy and lovely smile. I like you," he said.

I grinned, "Thank you."

As we reached my parents' house, he said, "I had a great time and I would love to get together again."

Then, when he arrived and stopped the vehicle in front of the house, he got out first and opened the door for me. He gave me his hand and I came out as I felt his warm soft hand. I liked his chivalrous classic behavior.

Then, we smiled at each other and I said, "I have to go."

"Oh, not yet!"

Then, he said kissing me on the cheek, "It was a pleasure having dinner with you."

I walked inside the house while Edward got into his vehicle and drove away. Edward had made a good impression on me.

I smiled. Edward had shown me that he was falling for

me during dinner, but I just wanted him as a friend even though I felt good being with him. Also, there was Pierre for whom I felt a great attraction.

CHAPTER XLI

Days later, during the following week, I saw Edward several times while he read the news on Channel 5 television. One day, while dining with my family, I suddenly felt I liked Edward when I saw him reading the news. I knew this was causing a problem because Pierre was still present in my life and I saw him almost every day. But Edward had me more interested in him than I expected.

"Do you like him?" Yannette asked.

"Why?" I said.

"You're not eating, you're just looking at him!" she said, smiling.

"I've eaten a lot." I said smiling, looking at my plate.

The others looked at me with curiosity and my other sister said aloud,

"It seems that Victoria fell in love with a Chilean man."

"Edward is friendly and affectionate, but I don't think I have fallen in love with him yet. There is also Pierre, who likes me very much," I said, trying to divert attention from them.

When Edward finished reading the news on television, he hurried home. That afternoon, he drank whiskey, realizing that my refusals to go out with him were due to his being a friend of Pierre. He had my phone number but did not dare to call me. When he finally got the nerve to call me, his cellular rang. I was calling him.

"Hello Edward! I'm Victoria."

"How are you, Victoria?"

After we said hello, I told him I had seen him several times on the news on Channel 5.

"Did you like the program?" Edward asked me with a loving voice.

"Yes, and you seemed very nice."

Moments later, we talked about the novel I had written. Then, he offered me help to publicize it. That had been one of the reasons why I had called him. We agreed to get together the next day to discuss the issue.

CHAPTER XLII

The next day before lunch, Edward picked me up at the house. When we greeted with a kiss and a hug our eyes met and I felt an enormous energy of love around me while in his mind he did not have any doubt that I was the woman he would like to spend with the rest of his life. During the ride, we spoke excitedly. We decided to go to Viña del Mar. I accepted knowing that in this trip Pierre could see me and I was risking my tranquility. I also thought that if Pierre saw us, it would create a serious problem between them. However, my desire to be with Edward was much stronger than my fears of Pierre. That day, I wore a pink dress, a long beige coat, and high heeled beige shoes. He looked very attractive and tall in his dark suit and white shirt. Even though we were almost the same height, he looked a little taller than I. During the trip, we talked about my novel. Then, on the radio, a romantic song that I liked began to play. Edward came up to me and tried to kiss me, his blue eyes looked seductive.

I turned away even though that day he was the ideal man for me. I liked him and I was happy to be with him. I was forgetting Pierre. I felt protected and loved by Edward. I liked his English presence, since he had been born in England and studied at the University of Cambridge. His innocent baby face, his blue eyes, and blond hair fascinated me.

"Darling, what happened?" Edward said.

"Nothing."

"You turned away from me, darling."

"No," I smiled.

"Yes, darling," he said lovingly.

He slowed down and leaned towards me. He tried to kiss me again.

"You had better watch the traffic. It's dangerous," I said.

"There is hardly any traffic."

He knew I liked him.

"It would be better if we got to know each other a little bit better. Besides, there's Pierre. . ."

"Pierre," he said with disappointment.

"We should get to know each other better," I said.

"Victoria, please, I loved you from the very first day I saw you. Pierre will understand. . ."

"Pierre is in love with me."

He felt angry as jealously toward Pierre passed through his mind.

We drove in silence for a while, then when the radio began to play a song that I liked, "Love Is Blue," I remembered a cognitive experiment on memory that I had conducted at Cambridge University.

After a silence, Edward took a deep breath and said softly returning me to reality, "What's the matter?"

"I was thinking," I replied.

"Can I know what you were thinking about?"

"A cognitive experiment on memory that I conducted years ago at Cambridge," I said.

"How interesting!" Edward said curiously.

Before arriving at Viña del Mar, Edward stopped the vehicle and parked on the shoulder of the road. He tried to kiss me again. This time, I let him. I liked his kisses. I felt good with him. I was forgetting Pierre.

It had started to drizzle and the road was wet. The leaves of the trees swayed in the breeze. From time to time, we saw people on the side of the road who walked with umbrellas.

When it stopped drizzling, he took my hands in his and said,

"Aren't you going to teach me how to conduct cognitive experiments on memory?"

"Yes, of course! Why not?" I smiled.

"How would you differentiate sensory perception from cognitive perception?" Edward asked me with curiosity.

"One is through the senses while the other is through the intellect," I said smiling.

"Darling, you fascinate me," Edward said leaning and kissing me. I could no longer resist him because he liked me so much.

After a while, we arrived at Viña. In the streets and avenues, there was a lot of traffic and many people were walking along the sidewalks. There were a lot of shops with their display windows. We looked at both sides of the street. Ahead, we stopped in front of a restaurant.

"Let's eat something!" Edward said.

"Are you hungry?" I asked.

"Yes, my love," he said. "I didn't have breakfast today."

A parking attendant opened the doors of the vehicle for us, and then he parked it. Talking, we walked as friends to the restaurant. He insisted that we walk hand in hand, but I told him to wait a bit. I was afraid that Pierre or some of his friends could see us. I would not know what to say to him. I also feared that the news could appear on a cover of a gossip newspaper *Farandulero* with us hand in hand.

Inside the restaurant, Edward could not take his eyes off me.

"You look adorable," he whispered over my shoulder.

In seconds, a waiter guided us to a table by a large window facing the ocean. After we sat down, he took the order. Edward and I ordered the same food. For lunch, we ordered roast chicken with mashed potatoes and lettuce salad and white wine. The restaurant was very romantic with candles in each table and silverware that shone on the maroon tablecloth. After we spread the napkins on our laps, we enjoyed the food. The classical music in the background was very romantic. I noticed that we felt mutual attraction and complemented each other in terms of personality and many other things. We were the most elegant couple in the restaurant.

"The food tastes very good," he said.

"I love it."

Before we had apple pie and vanilla ice cream for dessert, he asked me,

"How do you want me to publicize your novel?"

"Introducing me as a writer on your television program," I replied.

"It's an excellent idea," Edward said. "If you wish, I'm at

your disposal".

We agreed that he would present me on his television program to promote my novel. Edward often took my hand and said, "I like you very much, darling."

"Hmm," I smiled.

After lunch, we left the restaurant talking. Outside, we walked holding hands through some streets in Viña while we talked with excitement. The cool breeze shook my hair around my shoulders. On both sides of the street, palm trees rustled when the wind swayed their leaves.

Ahead, there was a green bench and we sat there. At that time, he took my hand and placed it between his and then kissed me. For a while, we talked as we saw people go by. Then, we returned to the vehicle holding hands.

"I love you, darling," Edward said putting his arms around me.

It had not been a long time since we had met, but I felt happy with him. He made me feel whole and most of the time I smiled when I was with him. We felt crazy in love with each other. I thought he was the right man with whom I would like to spend the rest of my life with. Sometimes, I tried to visualize how our children would be. Pierre was already like a shadow fading over time.

Before dusk, we returned to Santiago. On the way, we talked excitedly. Then, as we approached Santiago, he told me to go to his home. We went there for a while and sat on sofas in the living room. The living room and dining room with high ceilings had marble floors. Through the window opening to the terrace, I saw a beautiful garden. After talking a bit and drinking orange juice, I said standing,

"Why don't you take me home?"

"No, not yet," Edward said excitedly holding my hand and guiding me to the stereo. "Do you like to tango?"

"Yes," I said smiling.

Edward put a CD in the stereo and we started dancing the tango. I felt happy in his arms.

A while later, he hugged me and kissed me as we looked out the window. Then, we fell on a couch embracing and kissing while Edward unbuttoned my pink dress. I was feeling all the bliss, excitement, and longing as a result of the neurotransmitters dopamine, norepinephrine, and oxytocin as he whispered and caressed me passionately. His testosterone and endorphins seemed to be jumping. We made love as the sound of rain came in through the terrace. Edward and I was not a love at first sight, but now I felt that I loved him. We both felt a strong attraction, attachment, and happiness being together. I was very happy with Edward. Then, we laughed when we saw that our clothes were all over on the floor, chairs, and table. Later, we gathered our clothes and got dressed. I told Edward that I had to go, but he tried to keep me there.

Then, I asked him to give me a ride home, but he wanted me to stay with him. I convinced him to take me home. When we got there, I could see that Pierre was waiting for me, standing beside his car. I became pale. My heart beat with an intensity new to me. The moment I feared so much was happening. When Edward got out of the vehicle, Pierre rushed at him shouting that he was a bad friend and he had betrayed him. Edward did not have time to say anything. Pierre punched him in his face. Then, I saw both of them rolling on the ground punching each other. I could not believe what I was seeing. I did not want it to have ended this way. I tried to separate them, but it was impossible. The fight ended only when attracted by the shouts and blows, two of my brothers came out of the house and managed to separate them after a tremendous effort. Pierre shouted like a madman while Edward remained silent. The clothes of both were ripped. I did not know where to hide. My brothers helped Edward to stand up and took him to the house to put some medicine on his wounds, especially on the nose that was severely bruised, because of the fight. Pierre stood, shaking with anger and went to his vehicle and shouted at me, "I would never have expected something like this from you," I became pale. I thought that, in a sense, Pierre was right. Nevertheless, I would never have expected him to refuse to talk and understand our situation. I did not like that, without a word, he assaulted Edward. I walked slowly to the house and I started to help Edward. In spite of feeling sorry for what had happened, I felt relieved. I could no longer bear to keep a love affair with two men simultaneously. My family did not mention anything about what had happened.

When Edward felt better, he said, "Darling, I have to go." He embraced me and I could feel his warm chest as he kissed me. Then, Edward said he was going to call me, and then he left.

CHAPTER XLIII

I was awake at sunrise the next morning, miserable thinking about the previous day. The more I remembered the fight, the more nervous I became. But then as I was thinking about Edward, he called me on my cellular and told me he was dying to see me. Without Edward, I felt lonely. I felt the need to be with him. Then, I went to his home. When I arrived there, he ran to me and took me in his arms telling me with a kiss, "I love you, darling." His eyes shone with love for me.

"I'm the happiest man when I have you in my arms!" Edward said.

Embraced, we walked into the living room. There, we sat on the white couch where we made love before. For a while, we chatted as we had breakfast. I noticed he had a swollen face where Pierre had beaten him. After breakfast, we walked to the garden.

"It seems like spring, my love," Edward said while we listened to the chirping birds in the trees around the pool.

"Is spring your favorite season?" I asked.

"Darling, when I'm with you all the seasons are my favorite ones," Edward said embracing me.

Then, while we enjoyed eating chocolate with almonds, walking hand in hand through the garden, next to a rosebush, I jumped with fright when a rabbit suddenly crossed the path in front of me.

"Love, it was just a rabbit," Edward said, smiling.

"Yes, my love, but I thought it was a snake," I laughed.

Edward could not believe that there was a rabbit in the garden of his home. Sometime later, when we walked by the side of another rosebush, the rabbit appeared again. Edward followed him to a tunnel where he hid. As he touched him with a stick, all of a sudden, many small rabbits came out hopping.

"Ha, ha, ha," I laughed while some bunnies passed over our shoes. Giggling, I picked one up and smiled with excitement as I pet it. Then, we sat on the grass under an apple tree. The other rabbits hopped and jumped away sniffing with their trembling noses to another rosebush. Edward and I continued petting one. At first the bunnies had disappeared, but then they reappeared and peered through the rosebush.

The next week, Edward publicized my novel on his television channel and other channels also called me to interview me. In the newspapers and radios I also publicized it. Some people were surprised that I had taken the time to write the novel after having been so long in the United States. I told them that even though I spoke Spanish with a North American accent, I still continued loving my country.

CHAPTER XLIV

A few days before returning to the United States, my romance with Edward reached its climax, when he invited me to go to Viña del Mar at the home of one of his aunts. The house was unoccupied at the time. There, he proposed to me.

That evening, we sat on white sofas in the living room and talked embraced listening to romantic music.

"My love, stay and don't return to the United States," Edward begged me.

"I have commitments there, darling"

"Forget your commitments there and marry me."

"It's too fast, I need more time."

"I don't want to separate from you, darling."

"Let's wait a little longer."

He sighed and I did not know how to let him understand that I wanted to stay and be with him, but I wanted to wait a little longer.

After a short silence, I said, "I'm sorry."

"Don't apologize." he said.

Edward was frustrated by my unwillingness to be his wife so quickly. I felt I loved him and I really wanted to be his wife, but another part of me told me that it was too fast. We could hear the pattering of the rain coming from the terrace.

"Let's get married in secret and then later we tell everyone about it," Edward said caressing my hair with his soft hands.

"No. I wouldn't do such a thing."

"If you love me, stay!" Edward said.

"I love you, but let's wait a little longer."

"I'd be lost without you."

"You can call me every day."

"But it isn't the same as being married."

Then, he opened a bottle of champagne, filled two glasses and said,

"Let's toast for the triumph of our love."

He drank the glass of champagne dry while I sipped mine. After we drank a glass of champagne, we stood and walked to the window. He hugged me from behind while we talked. Sometimes, Edward turned my face towards him to kiss me.

"I'm in love with you," Edward said.

"Mmm," I murmured.

"I adore you, darling!" Edward took my hand and led me to a couch. We sat down and he pulled out something from his pocket. "I have a gift for you my love." When he opened it, I realized it was a ring.

"My love for you," Edward said with his eyes full of happiness.

"Oh, Edward, my love!"

Putting the ring on my finger, he told me, "Victoria, would you marry me and be my wife?"

"Edward, my love," I said happily, but a little anxious as he kissed me.

"I love you, darling, and I want you to be my wife!"

"Edward, I love you, but I have to return to the United States."

Edward put on the ring, but I said we had to wait until I return from the United States because I wanted the wedding to be a special event as it had been for my other married sisters.

That evening, we looked at some family pictures and then lay down on chaise lounges by the pool deck. Then, we walked upstairs to the living room and Edward turned on the stereo as he asked me if I liked music. After he kissed me while listening to music, we walked to the balcony and looked across at the ocean. The palm trees rustled in the garden.

At night, we went to have dinner at one of the most luxurious restaurants facing the ocean. We sat down at a round table for two by the window. It was a very romantic. The silver candelabra with a candle in the middle matched the silverware. The flame of the candle made our faces look pink. As we waited for the food, he said, "I love you." I smiled and said, "So fast." He told me that he fell in love with me the first time he saw me while I thought I was falling for the right man. That day, we had steak with boiled potato and lettuce salad. For dessert, we had peach pie. As we ate and talked with excitement, we often smiled with the pure joy of being together. From time to time, we looked at the lights of some ships across the ocean through the big windows. At the restaurant, there was a casino, but after dinner we preferred to go home. On the way there, he kissed me as we spoke lovingly.

"You're the only woman for me in this whole world," he whispered.

I smiled and said, "Do you really mean it?"

He took my hand and kissed it saying, "Yes, my love."

Back home, he switched on the lights and said hugging me passionately and leading me to a sofa, "I love you." As he kissed me, he rubbed his body against mine and then kissed me again. I felt tingling in my entire body.

"Do you like my kisses?" he whispered.

"Oh yes, I love them."

My body could not lie that I felt him deeply as he sighed with pleasure.

Then, we took a bath in the jacuzzi. He looked at my naked body and said, "You look very beautiful!"

I giggled and said, "You're also in very good shape."

He wrapped me around his arms and kissed me over and over as we bathed.

Then, we sat in the bed talking.

"I fell in love with you the first time I saw you," he said putting his arms around me.

"I found you arrogant the first time I saw you, but then I began to like you when I saw you reading the news on TV."

"Don't say that you didn't feel the same the first time you saw me," he said making love to me.

Smiling I murmured, "Yes."

"I love your sensuality, my love," he said as he kissed me all over as my hormones jumped up and down with desire.

That night, we almost did not sleep at all loving each other. Almost at sunrise, we fell asleep embraced and woke up when the sun was coming through the window. We felt very happy in each other's arms.

We got up at lunchtime and we prepared lunch. After we ate, we went for a walk around the beach.

"Do you often exercise?" I asked.

"Oh, yes, I jog, swim, and play golf on weekends."

"Why don't we jog, honey," I said.

"Now?"

"Yes."

"But, first give me a kiss."

I kissed him and he tightened his arms around me. Then, we jogged around the beach. It was cold that day, but we felt hot as we jogged. It surprised no one that we were in love.

Then, when it started to rain, we went back home.

At dusk, we returned to Santiago. Edward wanted me to spend the night at his home, but I told him to take me to mine. We agreed to get together the next morning.

Edward was my true love, and the man who completed me. I had fallen in love with him. Edward and I were very happy in each other's company. We missed each other when we were apart. He wanted that we lived together, but I told him that we should wait a little longer even though I was in love with him.

CHAPTER XLV

The next morning, I got up early to revise the plan of publicity for my novel, and then get together with Edward. After I revised it, I changed clothes to go out with him, but before doing so, I received a bouquet of roses with a card from Pierre asking me to continue our romance, since he still continued loving me very much. With disgust, I threw the card away in the trash container and happily hurried to meet Edward. I smiled thinking he was the love of my life and thought that I would never be happy with another man.

Edward greeted me with a kiss and a hug. Then, talking, we walked to the living room where my mom, sisters and brothers were talking. After breakfast, I showed Edward the library on the second floor. As we walked looking and opening books, I told Edward that many of these books had been read by generations of my family. He told me that he had been born in England and that people there often had libraries like ours.

That day, Pierre was anxious with the hope that I would respond to him, but I had forgotten him completely. As the hours passed without receiving an answer from me, Pierre became more furious and jealous. But, the hours passed and he did not hear anything from me. Night fell when Pierre began to think of taking revenge against me because he felt betrayed after I told him that I loved him. Some of my brothers had told me that Pierre seemed to be impulsive and very jealous, so he could hurt me, but I did not let it bother me.

Edward and I had lunch with my family. In the evening, Edward and I went to dinner at an intimate restaurant because we wanted privacy. The restaurant had silver candlesticks on each table. As we sat at the table next to a window overlooking the garden, Edward looked at me with passion. Inside, there was a romantic and intimate atmosphere, which we loved.

"What will you be having?" a waiter asked.

Looking at the menu, we ordered lobster with tossed greens, white wine, and fresh fruits for dessert.

"I love you, Victoria," Edward told me with a seductive smile.

I smiled back at him and said, "Will you go to the U. S. when I return there?"

"Yes, my love," Edward said holding my hand and kissing it.

His eyes filled with tears and mine too. Then, I noticed him being thoughtful.

"What are you thinking about?" I asked.

"About our love," Edward said.

He had fallen in love with me as I with him. I spent that night with Edward at his home. For a while, we kissed and embraced in the living room on the first floor. Then, we went upstairs and walked through the hallway to the living room balcony. From the balcony, we looked out as Edward held me around my waist kissing me. Then, we went to the bedroom and put on Indian enchanting music. We fell on the bed kissing as he lifted my sweater and kissed me around my breast. Then, he slipped my pants down and put his hand under my panties. As he caressed me, I felt his hot breathing in my ear.

"Do you like it?" he asked.

"Mmm," I said as the enchanting music increased my happiness with Edward.

I felt shivering with desire in my entire body and could not resist his love.

We fell asleep embraced. Next day, I woke up as he caressed my hair and looked at me passionately.

"Oh, darling," I said smiling.

"I'm so happy with you," he said kissing me.

I also felt very happy with him and that made me think about not returning to the United States, but then my reasoning told me I had my work there and had my plane ticket.

During that week over lunch, we told my family about our romance. They agreed and began to behave with Edward as another member of the family. Sometimes, Edward stayed at our house, but slept in one of the guest bedrooms.

CHAPTER XLVI

The day before my book presentation and signing of autographs, there was a terrible storm. It rained so much that the streets looked like rivers that dragged everything in its path. The windows of the mansion shook with the rain and the wind. The editor called me and said it would be best to postpone the presentation and signing of autographs. I had to travel to the United States that week. We decided that I would return to Chile in December for that event.

On TV channels, journalists showed many images of the flood.

The day before I left for the United States, I had dinner with Edward at his home. As we ate, he felt miserable and desperate when I told him I was returning to the United States the next morning at nine thirty.

"Don't leave me, my love!" Edward said.

"I can't stay, I have commitments!" I said.

"Love, if you go, I'll die," he said with his voice cracking as he blinked to release a tear.

"Don't say that," I said with tears in my eyes.

"I want you beside me. For me, our love is not a passing summer love."

When we finished dinner, we went to sit on a couch. Edward hugged me and tried to convince me to stay and get married.

"We'd go on honeymoon to England. The reason of my existence is you my love," he whispered tenderly but a little anxious.

"Wait until I come back in December," I said trying to convince him to wait and not lose hope in me.

"I'll not be happy without your love, darling," Edward said very sadly.

Suddenly, I told Edward that I had to return home, but he wanted to keep me and not let me go so far. Also, It seemed too long for him.

"No . . . don't go yet my love!" Edward said trying to stop me.

He hugged me and kissed me saying loving words, but then I convinced him to take me home. It was still raining.

We ran to his vehicle in the patter of the rain. When we got in, I said,

"I'll come back, my love."

Edward kissed me and we headed home. The mansion of the man I loved was left behind us, but I was sure that I would return. On the way there, Edward thought I would say that I could stay in Chile and would not return to America, but I said nothing.

Soon we got home, we said goodbye with a kiss and agreed to meet there the next morning to go together to the airport.

That night, I went to bed immediately. I had already packed my things in the morning. While Edward drove to his house, he felt sad and shed tears when he thought desperately that it would be the last night he would see me. He thought that I could find another man in the United States. That night, Edward set his alarm clock so as not to oversleep. Then, he went to bed. He could not fall asleep tormented about me going to the United States.

CHAPTER XLVII

After having stayed in Chile for some months, I returned to the United States. That morning was beautiful. The sky was clear and the breeze was a little cold. My family gave me a ride to the airport. Edward was going to meet us in our house to go there together, but I did not know what had happened to him because he did not come or even called. At the airport, we got out of the Range Rover and walked inside. By loudspeakers, the airlines announced the departures of flights to different places. My flight would leave at nine-thirty.

Meanwhile, I checked my bags at the airlines counter. We still had about an hour to say goodbye. We continued talking. We went to sit at a table and ordered some juice.

I heard through the speakers, "Passengers, your attention please, American Airlines announces the boarding of Flight 900 in an hour to the United States"

"Let's go to the boarding gate," I told them.

"The plane is leaving in about an hour," one of my

brothers said.

"Do you have your ticket?" Yannette asked.

"Yes, I have it."

When we saw the pilots and flight attendants of the plane, we became sad. We looked at each other tearfully.

When Edward awoke, it was nearly nine o'clock. The alarm did not go off. He jumped out of bed, got dressed quickly, and then rushed to the airport in his vehicle. Although it was late, Edward prayed to get to the airport on time. In his vehicle, he sped dangerously passing other vehicles that were also going to the airport. After he parked, he ran like a madman through the corridors of Pudahuel Airport. He had fallen madly in love with me and had to see me before leaving.

When they announced for the last time that passengers had to board the plane that was taking me to the U. S, we stood and walked to passport control. When I was walking to check in, I heard someone shouting my name. I turned around and saw Edward running through crowds of people, shouting, "I love you, love you, *mi amor*, Victoria."

I smiled with tears when I saw him and I said, "Edward, my love. I thought something had happened to you."

Edward took me in his arms and said, "I love you, *te amo*, and I'll wait until we get married."

"Yes, my love," I murmured as my tears fell on his cheek.

Edward embraced me tightly.

"I must go, my love," I said trying to free myself from him, as Edward did not want to let me go.

"I'll return my love and I'll take your kisses with me," I said and left quickly without looking back, while he, my mother, my sisters, and brothers looked at me with tears in their eyes. Then, they quickly rushed upstairs and saw the plane taking off and then it was very high and disappeared in the distance. With the sound of the plane that took me to the United States, they returned home.

Edward was brokenhearted. The return from the airport was a torture for him. He went for some time to the home of my family and then quickly returned to his home. Back in his home, he walked straight to his bedroom and lay down on his bed brokenhearted. He felt alone and empty as flashes of memories of our love crossed his mind. He remembered when we made love the first time and he held me close and he kissed me over and over. Then, he smiled as he looked at a photo of me and him. Then all of a sudden, he imagined me in the airplane and then when we were together. As he looked around, telepathically, he tried to transmit loving thoughts and feelings to me while in the airplane I thought lovingly about him. I tried to think why I had fallen so hard in love with him. He thought how I could feel and think what he was experiencing. He went to the kitchen and poured whiskey into a glass to ease his despair. He got drunk thinking I would be far away from him for many months. We had known each other for just a little while but he loved me as if he had known me for a long, long time. I also felt the same. I missed Edward and from time to time I smiled as memories with him crossed my mind.

I got to Dallas Fort Worth International Airport in Texas, the next day at dawn. After the plane landed, I walked down a long corridor that led to the Customs counters and passport checking.

"Welcome to the United States and enjoy your stay," an immigration officer said.

I had no problems. So I went to baggage claim to get my

bags. After I got them, I walked down the hall and left the airport and went to a hotel. I had about five hours before the flight to Honolulu, Hawaii. It was very hot, because it was summer in the U. S. and winter in Chile. I perspired because I was wearing a leather jacket, a sweater, pants, and white boots. At the hotel, I went to a shop and bought summer clothes. When I got hungry, I went to the restaurant at the hotel. I walked with a small bag and my purse. At the restaurant, I ordered something to eat. While I ate and missed Edward, a gringo looked at me, but I made it seem as if I had not noticed him because I was very much in love with Edward.

Two hours before the flight, I returned to the airport, which was very beautiful. I walked under the high ceiling. The marble floors and the airlines granite countertops shone. The bathrooms were spectacular. I thought it was one of the most modern airports compared to the international airport in Los Angeles, which is one of the oldest.

About one o'clock, I took the flight to Honolulu. When I arrived there, the day was beautiful. But, on the freeway, it started to drizzle. Then, as I was reaching Waikiki, the drizzle stopped and the sky cleared. Back in my apartment, I opened the large sliding doors to the balcony. A maid had cleaned it.

"My apartment is beautiful, classic style, and large. It's like a big house, and I love it," I said lovingly as if my apartment had been a child.

The building had a tremendous pool and landscaped gardens, two tennis courts, and many palm trees around.

Then, I went to see my Range Rover. It was covered with dust. When I drove, I felt it a little sluggish.

That afternoon Edward called me and said, "I love you and I miss you very much, darling."

"Me too, my love."

He said he was not happy without me and that he could not wait for me to return in December. I also felt the same.

In the evening, I met many of my friends. Some of them did not know what had happened to me because I suddenly disappeared. I told them about the death of my father and they offered me their condolences.

"How was the trip?" They asked.

"Very good," I replied.

That evening, we swam in the pool. I agreed to play tennis with my friends on the weekend in the building where I lived.

The next week, I resumed my work as a psychologist. On Monday, in my office, I sat behind my desk and looked at the list of my patients for that day. Then, my first patient who reminded me of Edward came in. He was depressed because his girlfriend had left him.

During my time in the United States, Edward called me almost every day. Also, I often talked with my family. Periodically, I communicated with the editor to discuss the novel.

I did not see Edward or my family for several months until my return to Chile. Often I reread the novel and found it more interesting. The editor and I added more chapters. The more I read it, the better I found it. In that way, I spent unforgettable hours immersed in the world of my novel.

CHAPTER XLVIII

Happily, at last in December of that year, days before Christmas, I not only returned to Chile to launch my novel to which I had added more chapters to honor my father, but also to be with the man I loved, Edward. That sunny morning, when summer had just started, I smiled happily when I arrived at the airport, Arturo Merino Benitez. I thought the airport was full of people for Christmas, but there were many of my fans who knew I was arriving that day and wanted my autograph. Months before, my novel had been publicized. When one of my male fans saw me, he shouted running towards me, "There she is! There she is!" Then, other fans followed. When they reached me, I smiled with excitement as I said, "Hola, my friends! Hello!"

They hugged me and kissed me on my cheeks. Then, they asked me for autographs. After I signed some books for my fans, I made my way to meet Edward and my family who were waiting for me. I have told them I was going to arrive that day, but the crowd did not let me see them. After some time, I was delighted when I saw them. Edward with my family rushed to greet me as I made my way to them.

"I love you and I adore you, darling," Edward let out a cheerful laugh as he swept me up in his arms and kissed me. His eyes brimmed with happy tears. He did not want to let me go to greet my family but then he did.

"Hello, daughter how was your trip?" my mom ran to greet me. My brothers and sisters followed her.

Edward looked very elegant and handsome in sportswear. My mother and sisters had overcome their grief and their eyes looked bright. My nephew, Alexito, had married Prisila and was holding his baby daughter Catalina in his arms.

"Auntie Victoria, here's your niece, Catalina!" my nephew said full with excitement.

"Hello, beautiful baby Cati!" I said holding her in my arms happily as the baby touched my face with her baby hands.

Then, we walked to the parking lot talking. Edward could hardly believe I was there again.

Edward and I left the airport holding hands next to my family.

Everyone was happy to see me again.

"I missed you so much, my love," I said happily as Edward embraced me.

"Tell me that you came back to marry me," Edward said to me.

"Yes, my love I came back to be your wife," I said with my eyes full of happiness.

"Oh, I love you and I want you to be with me forever," he kissed me excitedly.

"I feel the same, my love," I said.

That day, outside the airport, the green leaves of the trees swayed in the warm summer breeze.

Then, we got in the Range Rover and one of my brothers drove. On the way home, we talked and looked around.

"How happy I feel to be here!" I said.

Through the open windows of the houses along the road, we saw Christmas trees and children playing with toys on the sidewalk. As we passed Alameda Avenue, I smiled when I looked at the street vendors selling their Christmas toys. We heard children playing their horns in the street.

As we reached the mansion, through the open window, I saw some of my brothers walking next to the Christmas tree in the living room. When they saw me, they ran to greet me.

After we greeted with hugs and kisses, some maids walked behind us with the bags. The flowers and trees at the entrance of the mansion swayed in the breeze. That day was hot. The sun entered the hallway with high ceiling and marble floor.

"*Hola*, little sister!" Hugo said hugging me to greet me.

"Hello brother! How are you?"

"Happy to have you here," he said.

Some of the children ran happily into my arms to greet me. I took some of them in my arms. They told me they had done very well in their studies and that they wanted to speak English with me.

I walked toward the house with one child in one hand and another by the other. The children jumped and clapped their hands with the pure joy of seeing me.

"Auntie Victoria, how are you?" one child asked.

"Fine, thank you, and you?" I said.

After talking with my family and Edward in the living room, we had breakfast in the main dining room. While we had breakfast, we laughed with the joy of being together again.

When we finished breakfast, we relaxed for some time and then walked around the garden talking excitedly. The children jumped around the fountain in the middle of the garden that spread water to the flowers. The refreshing morning breeze shook the petals of flowers and green leaves of the trees.

"I'm very happy that you returned, my love," Edward said putting his arms around me and kissing me.

"I feel the same, my love," I said.

My family stared at us happily because they knew that Edward and I loved each other.

"We should go to the country estate in the South," I said.

"Yes, Victoria," my mother said.

"So, you can eat *soplillo*," Hugo said.

"Sister, Victoria, in the country, you will be able to eat all the meals that you love," said Roberto, who we called Titin.

"Yes, Titin," I replied.

As we walked by the side of peach trees, I took a peach, washed it, and I began to eat it.

"Aren't you going to give me a bit of peach?" Edward asked me.

I smiled and said, "Mmm. Come closer my love."

"It's delicious!" he said savoring a bite.

For a while, we sat on the grass in the garden. Then, it became lunchtime. There was a delicious smell of *empanadas*, meat pies with onions and roast beef coming from the kitchen. The laughter of the children was heard around while they played.

Then, we walked back to the house. In the kitchen, some

maids were frying *empanadas.* They had the habit of giving us some while frying them.

"Darling, the meat pie is very good, but very hot!" Edward said smiling.

"My love, let it cool and then eat it," I said.

"Yes, darling," Edward said.

"My children are used to eating meat pies as they're coming out of the frying pan," my mom said justifying the fact that we ate them without cooling them.

"A glass of wine?" Hugo said.

"Yes, meat pies are better with a good red wine," Edward said.

"Yes," I said smiling.

As we ate *empanadas* around the kitchen, some maids smiled at us.

One of them asked me, "How is the pie, miss?"

"It's very good!" I said.

Afterward, talking, we sat down to have lunch at the dining table of the first floor looking out at the terrace beside the pool. The children washed their hands before they sat down at a table next to ours.

The tables were covered with Christmas tablecloths. A beautiful silver candlestick matched the silverware. On the table, there was a tray with homemade bread and bottles of wine. My brothers, my sisters, my mom, and my in-laws and I spoke cheerfully.

"Victoria, the salad was prepared with vegetables from our garden," my mother said.

"It tastes very delicious!" I replied.

In the summer, we loved to eat vegetables from the vegetable garden.

During lunch, we agreed to go to the country estate in the South on the weekend.

After lunch, I suggested going to the garden.

"Okay," Yannette said and the others all agreed.

In a few moments, we were in the garden. The children were already there. We found them jumping and shouting cheerfully. We looked around in amazement. The children laughed when they saw a nest in a rosebush and the birds chirped as they peered out.

When it started to drizzle, we returned to the house. That evening, we went to the balcony of the dining room on the second floor. Before we started to have dinner, the drizzle stopped and we stood talking on the balcony. We looked across the pool and the garden that had some lamps. Edward had gone to his work on television Channel Five. When he came back from work, I watched him driving up through the driveway and then he parked under a tree next to the garden and walked toward the house singing.

When he came to the balcony, he greeted us with a kiss and then we sat to have dinner in the dining room. Then, we started eating. That day, dinner was delicious. We ate grilled lamb with mashed potatoes and tomato salad. For dessert, we ate peaches from our father's peach orchard. That night, the sky was covered with stars.

"Are we ready to go to the country estate?" Edward asked me.

"Yes, but I also have to prepare for the presentation of my book that will be next week," I said.

"Yes, darling," Edward said.

That night, we talked until late.

CHAPTER XLIX

Before the presentation of my novel, for the first time in many years I got up at sunrise happily to go to Yungay with my family and Edward. Thinking excitedly that Edward had spent the night in one of the guest rooms, I bathed and changed clothes quickly to be with him. That misty morning was refreshing. After some time, the mist disappeared. It was still dark. When I looked out from the balcony, I smiled when I saw Edward talking with some of my brothers and my mom in front of the terrace by the pool. We were going to have breakfast there.

"Hello, my love!" Edward said smiling when he found me looking at him.

Then, we left happily to Yungay. As we left the city, we talked. Later, the Range Rover entered the freeway called, "the Panamericana." There were not many cars at that time.

Ahead, we passed by Paine, on both sides of the road, there were various stalls selling peaches, watermelons,

melons, grapes, and *chicha*, which is like wine but sweet.

"Let's buy watermelons," Robert said.

"Yes, they must be very refreshing," I replied.

We stopped in front of one of the stalls and a vendor approached us.

"What can I do for you?" the vendor asked.

"We want watermelons," I replied.

"Yes, choose," the vendor said.

We bought many watermelons and melons. Seated at a table, we ate a refreshing watermelon and then continued our journey. Some people walked by the roadside. Later, the sun appeared and we saw some animals grazing on the fields on both sides of the freeway. At that time, the freeway was very crowded with vehicles.

Further ahead, we looked at the fields of wheat that were brown and animals with their young on both sides of the road. Later, we smelled *empanadas* from some houses along the road.

Hours later, as we drove from Chillán to Yungay, I looked around. The breeze moved the branches of the trees that were covered with green leaves. From time to time, we saw farmers walking through the pastures and we saw grazing animals.

We drove through many towns before arrived in Yungay. As we approached my family big country estate, we looked at the beautiful countryside when we came to the driveway and turned in. There were tall trees on one side of the drive. On the other were cherry, peach, and plum trees that were laden with fruit. Some workers who were working around greeted us happily. Then, there was our family's country mansion with its high white pillars. Some maids were cleaning the balconies upstairs. Through the open windows, we saw a

Christmas tree lighted in the living room on the first floor. Some workers were already up and were walking around the house and yard. When we tooted the horn, they came to meet us happily.

We greeted and then walked into the house and stood by the Christmas tree they had decorated on the first floor. The whole house smelled of the Christmas tree, which was the branch of a pine tree.

"Do you like the Christmas tree?" one of the workers asked.

"Yes, it looks very beautiful," my mother said smiling.

The workers had decorated the Christmas tree in the living room on the first floor right next to the window. For a while, we talked around the Christmas tree as the workers served us raisin bread with jam and fresh cow's milk. As we talked, the sun began to come in through the windows. All the classic furniture in the living room was familiar to me as a member of my family. Most of us wore jeans, a T-shirt, and sneakers. Then, we went upstairs to our bedrooms. The bedrooms were very big and sunshine streamed into them. When we opened the windows that opened to balconies, we saw the fruit trees that we could almost touch. Some birds were sitting in their nests.

After that, we went to the backyard. The warm breeze swayed the moistened flowers in the garden and in the pillars of the structure around the pool. For a while, we walked through the garden. There were some roses of many colors hanging from some trees and patches with carnations, daisies, pansies, jasmines, roses, bellflowers, and lilies. We enjoyed walking next to rosebushes and all kinds of roses climbing on the fences.

When we left the garden and then were near a vegetable garden, we saw some workers picking peas and beans. Others were cleaning the yard or preparing lunch.

"The vegetable garden looks bountiful!" I said happily.

"Yes, ma'am. Especially the peas," one of the workers said. "Your father loved to walk in the vegetable garden at this time."

"Yes, that's why we also like it," I said smiling.

"Victoria . . . today we're going to have chicken with peas soup for lunch," my mother said.

"Mmm, it's one of my favorite soups," I said smiling.

Ahead, John, a worker stopped his work and looked at us smiling and said,

"Miss, Victoria, your father would be happy to see you here."

"Yes, very happy," I replied.

John continued working.

"Good job," Robert, my younger brother, said.

The workers stopped working and grinned, "Thank you, and enjoy your walk."

We left them working and continued walking around.

Then, we returned to the house. The workers had set the table. We were hungry. That day we had a delicious lunch with chicken with pea soup, grilled lamb, and peaches and cherries for dessert.

"Mmm, the soup is very good!" I exclaimed, smiling.

"I'm happy you like it, Victoria," my mother said.

My brother Hugo had uncorked bottles of red wine and had filled glasses for each of us.

We felt the absence of our father as we ate. I thought about him and imagined him sitting at the head of the table.

At times, a cool breeze came in through the open window. "Sister Victoria, we're happy to have you here," Titin said. "Me too," I replied.

There was Christmas music playing in the background. After lunch, we went to the plaza. We met some friends and relatives there. Many families were walking with their children. We felt happy to see and hear a crowd of children singing and playing happily around a huge Christmas tree. We laughed when one of them with chocolate all around his mouth said, Feliz Navidad. All around us, there was a feeling of Christmas and the aroma of raisin bread. Many people baked their own raisin bread. We stayed there for some hours. And afterwards, we went home.

At dusk, we sat around the pool. We felt delighted as we talked and looked at the Christmas tree through the open windows. Soft Christmas music flowed through the balconies to the pool deck. Some of my brothers were walking on the second floor. When I thought about my novel, I went upstairs to the library to get a copy to reread it.

"Where're you going, darling?" Edward asked me when I stood up.

"To get my novel."

When I went back to the pool, I sat on lounge chairs next to Edward. The lanterns on either side of the pool lit up all around. Under the starry sky, watching the Christmas tree, we began to read the novel.

After we had read some chapters, we talked about them.

"If you had published the novel in winter, you wouldn't have shown these beautiful scenes," my mother said.

"Oh, yes!" I replied.

"The descriptions and characterizations are very

interesting," my sister Yannette said.

"Thanks," I replied.

"Next week begins the success of your novel, Victoria!" my mother said.

"I hope so, mom," I said.

Karincita's children blew their Christmas horns while they played around. They ran here and there happily.

The following morning, we got up before dawn to go to the farmhouse, which was about half an hour away. That morning, there was a cool summer breeze. While my sister Yannette drove, we looked at the countryside. We saw here and there patches of while flowers along the fields. Ahead, countrywomen dressed in faded clothing walked with their children along the road.

After some time, as we turned in to our country farm, the sun rose as we drove through the long driveway. On the left, there were fruit trees filled with fruits such as apples, cherries, peaches, and plums. On the right, there were sheep and goats grazing. A worker who was walking down the driveway greeted us very happily.

Then, we came out of the driveway, and there was our huge country mansion that was surrounded by gardens and chamomile. We parked the Range Rover in front of the mansion. The workers who were walking in the yard ran to greet us filled with excitement.

While we walked talking towards the entrance of the house, the maids walked behind us with the bags. We noticed the smell of animal manure coming from the stables. After we sat in the living room for a while, we agreed to go to the stable that was next to the tennis court. That morning we looked at the workers as they milked the cows in the stable.

They had made cheese the day before.

That morning, we had breakfast and then went for a walk around the farm accompanied by dogs. The dogs jumped on us occasionally. They liked to look at our faces. Then, we walked through the garden. The dew on the green leaves of the flowers and trees looked like crystals with the morning dew. The sun had begun to emerge. As we walked by the side of the tennis court, the door of the stable opened and a worker came out with a bucket of milk.

"Do you want fresh milk?" the worker said.

"Yes . . . It's very delicious," I said smiling.

We watched the cows for a while. Some calves were lying on the wheat straw. Then, we went to the stable of the sheep. The children ran to embrace the baby goats. I took them in my arms. We all loved and petted them.

Then we walked out of the stable and walked to a vegetable garden. The peas and beans were higher than us. Among them, we could see wildflowers. Butterflies flitted around us. We laughed, "Ha, ha, ha," when the shoots of peas and beans tickled us. That day, some of us wore shorts, jeans, shirts, tennis shoes, and hats.

"You'll have to get used to the country life, Edward," my mother said.

"I love everything that Victoria likes," Edward said.

"Mmm, do you really mean it?" I murmured, smiling.

"Yes, darling," Edward said kissing me.

As we walked, the children began to run ahead of us. In the fruit orchard, the tree branches almost touched the ground so full of fruits. Some of the children climbed a plum and an apple tree and started eating fruits like my brothers and I had done in the past. The children shouted with joy when they shook the plum trees. The plums fell and we picked them up happily.

"It's very sweet!" Edward said, savoring a plum.

"When we were girls we loved to climb these fruit trees," I said with excitement.

"Yes, you know these trees very well," my mother, said.

"Sometimes, we used a cattle prod to get apples that were on the high branches," Hugo said.

The next day, we got up at sunrise. We had breakfast with fresh cow's milk and cheese with homemade bread and marmalade. Then, we walked across the countryside and down to the wheat field. In the wheat field, we opened a path among the wheat straws. After a while, we laughed, as we stood deep in wheat. The brown wheat was higher than us and swayed with the refreshing summer breeze. There was the smell of wheat straw that we loved. The wheat straws were full and ready to be harvested. I thought maybe it was my father who made the wheat sway. The birds chirped around us. We did not care that the wheat straws were wet with dew and moistened our clothes. After some time, we were having so much fun running across the wheat and playing hide and seek that the children of the workers came and joined us. Then, the sun was very strong. Some of the dogs jumped and barked softly at our sides while others searched for the scent of partridges in the wheat. From time to time, frightened partridges ran through the wheat trying to fly when the dogs went after them. All of a sudden, we heard some children shouting hidden in the wheat despite the heat. Their faces and hair looked dusty. They ran to play with us.

At lunch, we went back to the house and then went to the little beach, a sandy area on the bank at the side of the river that was on our farm.

That afternoon, on the way to the little beach, the Range Rover raised dust that accumulated on our faces. All around, the trees were dusty.

At the little beach, we giggled behind some bushes as we put on our bathing suits and anticipated having fun. Then, we went swimming while a maid prepared lunch for us. I wore a green bikini that I had bought in the U. S. It was perfect against my pale skin. I looked slender.

"You look very sexy," Edward whispered in my ear.

That day the maids grilled lamb and as we swam, we smelled the grilling lamb and sometimes we looked at how it was browning.

After a while, we got hungry and went back to where the maids were grilling. We sat on the green grass under some trees and had lunch.

Then, from a tray, each of us took a glass of mote, which was peeled green wheat, and mixed it with peach juice.

"It's very delicious," I said.

"Mmm, yes, Victoria," Robert said.

"It's very good," Yannette said.

"Yes," Karincita replied.

"Like your aunts, you like the *mote con huesillo*," my mother said smiling.

I felt very happy in the countryside of my childhood. The vista of the river with tall trees with thick foliage and wild grass and flowers waist high looked lovely. After a while, we laid down on the green grass beside the river. When Edward put on sun tan lotion on my stomach, one of my sisters joked, "Edward, are you still going to be that lovingly when you marry her?"

We all laughed a little because Edward and I had not told them we were going to get married.

"I enjoy it now, so I should enjoy it in the future," Edward said.

Then, we jumped in the water again and laughed as we splashed water playfully.

"Our father loved to swim in this river," Yannette said.

"Your father was a very good swimmer," my mother said.

"From heaven your father sees you and protects you," a worker said.

"Yes," my mother said.

At night after dinner, we played the piano in the living room. When Edward played, *Besame, Besame Mucho,* we all sang with him and he kissed me when he finished playing it. We were so in love that we showed each other affection in many different ways.

The next day, at sunrise, we accompanied some workers to cut wheat to make the traditional *soplillo*. After we cut some wheat straws, we went back to the house with the bundles of wheat. In the driveway, under the shade of some tall lindens and cherry trees, we sat and started to shake the wheat straws and the young green wheat grains fell out. From time to time, we smelled the scent of peach marmalade coming from the kitchen.

That day we had *soplillo* for lunch. The *soplillo* tasted very good.

After lunch, we went to the peach orchard that our father had planted years ago. At the orchard, peach trees were filled with fruits. We got some and sat down on the grass under a tree to eat them.

"They're very sweet!" I said savoring one.

"Hmm, yes, Victoria," my mom said eating one.

"My father loved his peach orchard," Yannette said.

"Now, he must be watching how you enjoy his peaches," my mother said smiling.

'Yes, mom," Robert said.

From time to time, we heard the conversations of the workers who were harvesting the peas in the vegetable garden.

"Hello, the harvesting is very good!" one of the workers shouted cheerfully when he saw us.

My mom said, "Great! I like to hear that."

CHAPTER L

At last came, the long awaited day of the presentation of my novel and book signing. The titled of my novel was, My Father, The Legacy of an Enterprising Man. That beautiful sunny morning, I got up early. As I bathed and changed clothes, I smiled thinking how happy I would feel signing autographs. The publicity of my signing of autographs had been on television and newspapers. Also, it had been publicized at some universities, schools, and on the radio. After I had breakfast, my family, Edward, and I left the house excited for the presentation of my novel. The editor was waiting at the bookstore. Along the way, I felt a little nervous about the reactions of my readers. But my fears disappeared as we approached the bookstore and saw lots of people who were waiting to enter the presentation.

Edward parked the Range Rover in front of the bookstore. After he got out, he opened the door and gave me his hand as I stepped down.

"Victoria, we're waiting for you!" My editor said, smiling.

"Here, I am!" I said excited and amazed by the crowd.

After we greeted, we made our way into the bookstore. As we walked, I thought that everything was going better than I expected. Some people pushed one another for me to sign autographs or to tell me something about the novel. We passed many people.

Then, we went to the bookstore. Inside, it was crowded and people cheered when they saw me.

"I cannot believe that so many people came to the presentation of my book," I thought as I looked around smiling.

It was the success I desired.

Some journalists approached their microphones to ask me different things.

"What do you think about the success of your novel?" a reporter asked me.

"I feel very happy about it," I answered smiling.

Some youths wore caps and shirts with the title of my novel. Photographers focused their cameras on me and journalists of newspapers asked me questions.

At the beginning, I stood by my editor in front of a table full of copies of my novel. On the right, there was a Christmas tree. The editor, with a copy of my book in his hand, said,

"Let's give a warm welcome to the great Chilean-American writer, Victoria Wellington, author of the novel *My Father, The Legacy of an Enterprising Man.*"

Everyone clapped to welcome me. I smiled and greeted them affectionately,

"Welcome everyone to the presentation of my novel!"

Edward was there and most of my family and several

guests of honor, and friends. Only my family and guests of honor were seated on chairs. In the rear and both sides of the bookstore, many people were standing. They had reserved the bookstore especially for the event. From the ceiling hung a lamp that had a lot of bulbs. The entrance had large windows with publicity of my novel and Christmas decorations. On the walls were shelves full of books. Some shelves were moved to make more room for people. Inside, we smelled the scent of pines, coming from the Christmas tree.

After my editor introduced me, I turned to the crowd to tell them about me and about my inspiration to write my novel. Then, I left them with musicians who played classical music with violins, cellos, and basses. The crowd applauded when the musicians finished playing. Then again, I went to the crowd to tell them the story of my novel and to read some of my favorite scenes it. Before we toasted with champagne to the success of my novel, I asked if anyone had any questions. Many people asked me questions.

"What motivated you to write your novel?" a person asked me.

"The death of my father," I replied.

"Are you going to translate your novel into other languages," another person asked me.

"Yes, of course," I said.

After I answered many questions, I invited them all to have a toast. While toasting, some people congratulated me on the success of my novel. I had already distributed some copies of my novel in advance for reviews and universities. Then, I invited everyone to see and know my novel and to a buffet. In groups, they crowded around the table with copies of my novel. Some bought copies of my book and asked me to autograph them and write dedications and then they walked to the buffet. I was excited and very happy to sign one autograph after another as my fans congratulated me. My fans kept me busy signing autographs that I did not even have time to eat. I was very happy that my fans became so interested in my novel. I felt like a famous bestseller novelist.

Before the presentation of my book finished, I thanked them. The crowds cheered happily as they clapped their hands.

"I liked your novel very much," some people shouted.

"Great!" I said smiling.

Among the people waiting for me to sign their autographs, there was a worker from my father's country estate in the south of Chile. That surprise almost made me cry with emotion.

Through the door that was a little open, fresh air entered. Inside, there was air conditioning, but it was still hot.

The news of the publication of my novel was known throughout Chile, especially when reporters interviewed me live. They commented enthusiastically about the success of my novel and then asked me questions.

A reporter from Channel Five television where Edward worked interviewed me.

"Could you tell our viewers how you feel about the success of your novel?" the reporter asked me.

"Very happy and grateful for the welcome of my novel," I replied.

"I can see that," the journalist said with excitement. "What message would you like to give to the readers of your novel?"

"To continue enjoying them."

The camera was focusing on me while I answered some questions.

Then, the journalist approached a youth with his

microphone.

"What do you think about the novel?" the reporter asked.

"I really liked it very much," the youth answered.

A television screen, on a shelf full of books was showing the interview live.

The journalist smiled and asked me enthusiastically, "Can you tell us the title of your next novel?"

"Yes, but I prefer it to be a surprise," I said smiling.

"Could you tell us how long it took you to write it?" the reporter asked me.

"About a year."

"Do you think the novel can inspire Chileans to read?"

"Yes, absolutely," I said.

"The country needs people like you who care about improving the education in Chile," the journalist said.

People clapped and among the murmurs were heard expressions like, "We need people like you, Victoria, to write about our reality."

That afternoon when I finished signing autographs, I thanked the audience and then I tried to make my way out of the bookstore among crowds of people. Outside, children were playing their Christmas horns. Some people followed me. For a while, I answered questions to journalists and to some of my fans.

"Do you think the novel could be adapted to a movie?" one of my fans asked.

"Yes, of course."

"What do you think about the success of your novel?" another journalist asked me even though another journalist had already asked me the same question.

"I'm very happy."

A few minutes later we left the bookstore with my editor,

Edward, and my family and some guests and went to my parent's house to celebrate the success of my novel. The workers of the house had taken about a week to prepare the party. But the invitations had been sent about a month earlier. As we made our way out, some people threw me kisses with their hands. Others requested me for more autographs. Then, we headed to the mansion in my Range Rover. Waving my hand out of the window, I said goodbye to my fans who had attended the presentation.

Inside the vehicle, the editor hugged me smiling to congratulate me,

"You looked very happy signing autographs. Was it the success you wanted?"

"Yes, and thanks for having faith in me," I said.

"For a long time, no other writer had so much success as you, Victoria," he said enthusiastically.

"How long?" I asked with curiosity.

"Years."

Later the editor asked me, "When are you going to write your next novel?"

Once I published others I wrote in Spanish and English.

"Great!" the editor said.

That day was hot, but with the air conditioning we felt cool inside the vehicle.

"The book signing was much more successful than I thought," I said.

"My love, it was what you wanted so much," Edward told me with a kiss.

CHAPTER LI

As we approached the mansion, Edward stopped the Range Rover and asked one of the workers if his English friend had already arrived. Edward was waiting for him because he would be very important in the dissemination of the book.

"Yes sir, he arrived in a gold Range Rover."

"Thank you."

"You're welcome, sir," the worker said.

We moved on. Minutes later, we were inside the house with some guests.

That afternoon, back home, we saw some workers near the access gate, which was open to facilitate our entry. Some guests were arriving in their vehicles while others walked toward the front entrance. A worker greeted them with a bow and escorted them down a hallway to the big dining room on the first floor. After we got out and walked to the front door, the guests greeted me with a kiss and congratulated me.

Inside the house, we heard cheerful Christmas music

and conversations. When we reached the dining room, this seemed like a theater by the number of guests. At the center of the room, there was a huge Christmas tree. Big tables by the windows were covered with Christmas tablecloths. On the tables were roasts, salads, champagne, raisin bread, wine, and beverages, etc. On the white walls of the dining room were pictures of my family. Through the terrace, we looked at the blue pool surrounded by flowers and tall trees. The guests chatted in groups. Some talked about my novel. Others walked through the middle of the dining room around the Christmas tree. Others were near the tables. People, who did not eat standing up, sat around the tables. Inside, with so many people, it was very hot. The large windows were open. Some people had in their hands a dish with roast beef and salad. A few ate standing next to the tables.

Later when we noticed that all the guests had arrived, the editor proposed a toast to the success of my novel and took a bottle of champagne that was at a table and opened it. When the cork popped up to the ceiling, people laughed out loud to hear it splash. The editor filled some glasses. Then, the workers continued serving champagne and filling the glasses of the guests.

The editor looked at everyone and said loudly.

"Let's toast to the success of the novel *My Father, The Legacy of an Enterprising Man* by the writer Victoria Wellington."

We all raised our glasses and some of us touched them. The champagne was very refreshing.

"Another glass?" the editor said.

"Yes," some of us said and drank another glass of champagne.

The sun was coming through the window. That day was hot. After that, conversations, music, and laughter were heard throughout the house.

Later, I invited the guests to eat.

My editor and I approached a table. On a plate, we put a piece of roast beef with salad and went to sit at a table. We told a maid to bring us a glass of red wine. During the reception, the guests congratulated me on my novel. Some looked at the diamond ring that Edward had given me. That day, I was wearing a pink dress and a white hat that I had bought in the United States. A refreshing breeze entered through the open windows.

For a while, we talked to the guests who were sitting at the table that was next to the Christmas tree. When they stood, I went to talk to my mom and Edward. Edward wanted to be with me all the time, but I had to talk with everyone. Edward was very jealous, but not with my editor because he found him very English, gentle, and virtuous.

"Victoria, the guests compliment me for having a daughter who writes so beautifully," my mother said.

"Thanks mom."

My brothers, sisters, other relatives, and friends talked to me while we ate.

When I realized that the editor was alone standing looking at the Christmas tree, I walked towards him. For a while, we talked contemplating the Christmas tree. Then, we went to sit at a table that was next to the window. A reporter approached us, sat at our table, and said,

"I really liked the release of your novel."

"Thanks," I said smiling.

"Victoria writes with passion," the editor said.

Inside, we heard the buzz of conversations. Some talked, others laughed, and others continued eating. Christmas music was heard throughout the house.

I was aware of Edward watching me as I ate and talked to others, but I pretended that I did not notice it. When the editor began to talk with other people and I went to get more food, Edward came up to me.

"I love you," he whispered.

I smiled and said, "Oh, darling!"

Then the editor and I sat next to the Christmas tree. For a while, we talked with others who approached us. When we got hungry, we went to the table. We place strawberries with cream on plates and walked to the window.

"The strawberries taste very good," the editor said.

"Delicious," I replied.

Inside it was very hot. It was already dark. The windows were open, but it was still hot.

"Let's go to the balcony," the editor told me because he had to tell me something.

"Okay," I replied.

Before we walked upstairs, Edward introduced me to Roger Sperling, his English guest, also known by the editor. He was a very important person in one of the most prestigious universities in Chile. The editor was interested that I knew him. That is why he had invited him.

"Why are you so late?" the editor asked Roger.

"The traffic," Roger said. "You know how the congestion is at this time."

"Well. The important thing is that you arrived. Let's go to the table," the editor said.

Roger, the editor, and I sat at a table to talk.

Roger had told my editor that the university needed a classic Chilean novel like mine. Therefore, he wanted to tell me that. Then, as we talked, some people came to talk with us. In the dining room, we smelled fried onions.

To talk more quietly, my editor, Roger, and I walked through the crowd toward the second floor balcony. We left the room and entered the hallway to the stairs. Upstairs on the balcony of the dining room, we stood looking out.

"Your novel fascinates me," Roger said to me.

"I like to hear that," I said with excitement.

"I'm sure that students are going to love it," Roger said.

After we talked about my novel, we touched other themes.

"How beautiful is the starry night!" my editor said.

"Yes, very nice," I replied.

"It's hot inside," a guest said.

"Yes, but it's cool here," my editor said.

For a while, we talked leaning on the railing of the balcony. The warm breeze shook my long blond hair.

Later, we smelled roast beef. It made me hungry. I thought I was getting to be a glutton. The other guests returned to the dining room. Edward walked upstairs and kissed me when he noticed that we were alone.

Then, I went back to talk with my editor and Roger.

"How about if you sign autographs at the university this semester?" Roger said.

"Yes, I'd love it," I said.

"The department of literature wants you to sign autographs," the editor said.

"I'd like it very much!" I smiled happily.

"We already requested two thousand copies and the students cannot wait to read your novel," Roger said.

Then, a worker came to us to ask if we needed anything. In the dining room, again, we walked to the table and took chicken on a plate. A maid served us fruit juices. Around us, my family and guests talked excitedly. The chicken had been roasted on a fireplace and had a golden color.

Later, we ate raisin bread. From time to time I talked to the guests, but then again met with the editor. Inside, we heard the buzz of conversations and laughter. A while later, the editor and Edward talked while I talked to other guests.

Suddenly, I heard some murmurs as if people had been singing accompanied by guitars as I returned to meet with my editor and Edward.

"Do you hear singing?" the editor asked me.

"What?" I said a little puzzled.

"Do you hear some people singing?" my editor asked me again.

"No," I replied with curiosity.

For a while, we ignored the sound. We continued talking and eating. Then, when we heard that some people were actually singing, we hurried upstairs and from the railing of the balcony looked out. Some of the farm workers were singing with their guitars. The others followed. They were from our farm and had come to serenade me because of my novel. Then, the others felt fascinated listening to the serenade and looking at them.

Men, women, and children dressed in colorful clothes and ponchos sang happily celebrating the novel, My Father, the Legacy of an Enterprising Man. They played the songs that my father liked best. The song Cielito Lindo echoed through the entire mansion. A farmer opened many bottles of red wine and then filled some glasses and offered a toast.

"In honor of the patron who was so good with us!" they all raised their glasses.

Under the starry sky, we heard the folk songs the farm workers sang for us. Then, one after another they appeared in the dining room.

"I hope you liked the serenade," one of them said.

"Thank you very much, your *patron* must be very happy to have heard you from heaven," my mother said.

"Now, we have to go back to take care of the farm," one of the farmers said.

"Before you leave, eat something," my mother said kindly.

"Thank you very much, ma'am, but we have to return to the farm to work."

"Your, *patron* would be happy to see you eating after you came to give your respect with your serenade," my mother said.

"Okay, ma'am, it's still early."

They approached the table, ate and drank.

"The roast chicken is very delicious, but don't let it drip down your arms," one of the farm workers said to his son.

While everyone ate, drank, and talked, I said,

"Thank you very much to all of you for coming to the presentation of my book."

The editor and my family stood among the guests. On the four walls, there were large screens showing my family walking in the garden in summer time in the country mansion. Other screens showed the harvesting of golden wheat on our farm and horseback riding which was our favorite sport during the harvesting. On the right side of the wall, there was another screen showing the family decorating the Christmas tree when we were kids. My father used to say, "For Christmas we celebrate the birth of our savior Jesus Christ." In the scene, my father brought a pine branch in with the workers and us to the living room. My parents and some workers fastened tightly the pine branch in a container wrapped in colorful gift paper. Beside the high pillars at the entrance of the house facing the pool, we had placed the boxes with decorations. After a while, we moved the boxes next to the Christmas tree. We were kids. With excitement, we ran here and there with the toys we got from the boxes. Then, we all took out the toys from the boxes and hung them on the tree. After all the toys were hanging on the Christmas tree, we looked at it happily. My father had placed the baby Jesus on the top of the tree, "The glory of the Lord Jesus Christ shines among us, and today he was born to save us," my father used to say as we looked at the Christmas tree covered with Christmas lights like a starry sky.

In another scene, my parents, brothers, and I were under the Christmas tree opening Christmas gifts. We jumped happily. Some of my brothers played their horns, ate raisin bread, hugged one another, and compared the gifts.

Handel's symphonic music, "Messiah" and other children's songs and symphonic music were heard throughout the mansion with the family and guests celebrating.

Before the celebration finished, my family, Edward, and friends gathered around me to congratulate me and wish me good luck with my novels. Edward could not wait to kiss me and tell me how much he loved me. I felt really happy for their support and encouragement. To my surprise, when the guests were gone, Edward let out a cheerful laugh as he swept me up in his arms and kissed me, "I love you…" I felt very happy in his arms. My family looked at us and smiled. They knew that we loved each other very much. That day went by really fast celebrating the success of my novel.

PART IV

✵

CHAPTER LII

My life was quiet until one evening I received a phone call from Pierre that disrupted my tranquility completely. It was a huge surprise because it had been over two years since I had broken my romance with him. I even thought that Pierre had rebuilt his life with another woman. Since that day, Pierre's calls increased day by day. I tried to hide from Edward and conceal the anguish that those phone calls caused me because I did not want to break the harmony of my family. In the calls, Pierre told me he was going to kill Edward.

Although Pierre had threatened to hurt me for having left him, I continued my love affair with Edward and married him in Chile and we moved to Honolulu, Hawaii. There, we had a son called William. When our son was two, despite the threats Pierre had made to me, we visited my family in Chile. That day when we arrived, my family was waiting for us at the airport. Happily, we greeted and went to my parents' home in the Range Rover. It was a beautiful day, the sky was blue and the sun was shining. On the way there, we talked cheerfully.

"We're going to harvest the wheat," one of my brothers said.

"How exciting! When?" I asked.

"Tomorrow, but we're going there in a few hours," another said.

We talked cheerfully from the airport to the house. Over breakfast, we smiled in anticipation of the excitement we would have on the wheat harvesting in Yungay. Pierre's calls had faded away.

"The wheat must be waiting," I said.

"Yes, we're leaving in two hours," Hugo said.

"It's a wonderful day to travel to the south," my mother said.

Over breakfast, some workers placed the luggage in the Range Rover.

"The workers must be preparing the horses for us to ride in the countryside," Robert said.

"I haven't seen wheat harvesting in years," I said.

"We're going to have a great time," one of my brothers said.

After breakfast, we walked into the garden happily. The children had already run there and were having a lot of fun playing. Edward and I walked hand in hand, with my brothers, mom, and sisters laughing happily. As soon as we arrived at the garden that had many rosebushes, carnations, and impatiens, Willy who was playing with his cousins, shouted laughing with happiness, "Come!" We walked fascinated towards him. Our son was very spoiled and loved it when we took him in our arms.

All of a sudden, when I least expected it, I saw on the balcony on the second floor the figure of Pierre with a gun in his hand. My mind become confused at the time, the panic and surprise left me immobilized. Suddenly, like a loud thunder, Pierre fired his weapon and I felt Edward's warm hand slipping from mine. His body slumped next to me on the ground. Pierre had fulfilled his revenge and like a lightning, the threats I had received from him to which I had not given importance crossed my mind. I felt guilty. The whole world seemed to have crashed and fallen over me. Holding Edward tightly, I shouted desperately, "Edward, my love!" A piercing scream came from the deep inside of me and was heard in the entire mansion. "I love you, Victoria," Edward gasped with a sigh. He was dead in my arms as if he was protecting me from the rain. I could not believe that the love of my life was dead next to me. The others panicked and tried to pick him up crying and screaming, but Edward was dead with his eyes open.

When I looked up and I saw Pierre peering on the balcony of the second floor, I screamed crying, "Get him, he's upstairs."

Frightened, Pierre rushed into hiding, but some workers who had seen him ran after him. Quickly, they caught him and wrestled him to the floor, pinning his arms and legs so he could not escape. Then, they tied him up while waiting for the police to arrive, which did not take long.

The police handcuffed Pierre and read him his rights. Then, a police officer led Pierre to the van of the police investigators. He called his lawyer and was taken away in handcuffs to the headquarters of the Police Department to be there for questioning. I was sad and in shock but my rage was so intense that I wanted to kill Pierre with my own hands, but I knew I could not do that, but my anger was raging. Pierre waited there for his lawyer who took about fifteen minutes to get there to take the statements. By order of the prosecutor, the accused, Pierre, was detained in prison while other police officers and detectives took photographs and other evidence of Edward's body in the garden. Then, the detectives covered Edward's body with yellow plastic sheets. The police called the prosecutor who told him not to move the body until he came to the scene to take statements and establish the facts of the murder. Soon, officers of the Legal Medical Service arrived and took the body by order of the prosecutor to the Medical Examiner. Many journalists had come to report the crime scene live.

That evening, many friends and relatives were shocked when they saw the news on TV. To avoid further scandal, I did not answer any questions to any reporters. I felt guilty for the death of Edward. I never told him about the phone calls Pierre had made threatening us.

The day of the preliminary hearing, Pierre arrived in handcuffs with two prison guards next to him and left him sitting beside his attorney in front of the judge. When the trial began, the judge asked Pierre to identify himself. Pierre swore nervously in my presence as tears rolled down my face. After the presentation of the accused, his defense lawyer spoke and then my lawyer presented the evidence of witnesses and experts against the accused.

By order of the court, some detectives made a search of Pierre's home to further investigate evidence about the brutal crime committed by the accused. In this proceeding, detectives found several pieces of evidence implicating

Pierre, a plan of the house of my family with the details of the rooms, a report on where he bought the gun, pictures of me and a lot of letters he never sent, but showing his obsession of loving me and taking revenge on me.

Dr. Spain, as a forensic expert of the Medical Examiner Service, performed the autopsy and found that a nine mm bullet had pierced Edward's chest cavity, which was the same that was in the gun that Pierre had fired. Also, they found on the right hand of Pierre recent gunshot residue.

At the preliminary hearing, the judge said the parties were notified for the final judgment on Wednesday, October 15 of that year at ten o'clock.

Victoria's lawyer with all the evidence that she showed in the preliminary hearing was convincing to the judge at the hearing of the final judgment and closing arguments to dictate the crime as a premeditated homicide. Pierre was sentenced to forty years in prison. On hearing his sentence, Pierre shook and accepted his sentence and then turned around and with tears in his eyes apologized to me saying, "Forgive me, but don't forget that I'll always love you." Then, two guards took him away to serve his sentence in handcuffs, while I felt satisfied that justice was done, even though I would not see my love, Edward again.

It was about nine o'clock when I got out holding my son, William's hand thinking of Edward and hoping that someday William would know how much his father had loved him. I did not answer any questions to any journalists because I wanted to get back home quickly. As we drove back along Providencia Avenue to the mansion of my family, I opened the windows of the Range Rover and the sweet smell of blooming trees and sounds of birdsongs entered.

That spring morning, in the bright sunshine, and a warm breeze, with my son William and my family, I went back to the garden of the mansion again. Back in the garden, I missed Edward, but then I smiled with excitement as I looked across the flowers remembering wonderful times I had spent with him there. In my imagination, I saw Edward standing there holding Willy in his arms. Then, all of a sudden, I sighed and felt as if I had fallen into a dream as memories of Edward poured from my mind. The deeper I went into my dream, the happier and inseparable he became to me. I remembered when I was pregnant expecting Willy and we walked in this garden holding hands as he patted my stomach tenderly. I knew that he would want me to be very happy, but there would never be another Edward for me. Then, as we walked looking and smelling the sweet aroma of cherry, peach, and plum blossoms with pink and white flowers, bees buzzed around. Willy with his cousins laughed and shouted cheerfully as they played across the grass among the flowers, butterflies, and some rabbits that peered here and there. Now I just hope that my son, William, continues the traditions of his father and grandfather.

END

REFLECTIONS ON THE NOVEL
Questions

1. What does the title of the novel suggest?

2. How did you think it was going to end?

3. What do you think of the novel? Did you like it? Why?

4. What is your favorite scene? Why?

5. Who is the narrator?

6. How long is it between the beginning and ending of the novel?

7. Who is your favorite character? Why?

8. How would you have liked the novel to finish?

9. Who is Edward?

10. What do you like the most about the novel? Why?